PENGUIN BOOKS

CAN'T AND WON'T

'This is what the best and most original literature can do: make us more acutely aware of life on and off the page . . . In a universe drowning in words, Davis is a respite. What she doesn't say is as important as what she does' Peter Orner, *The New York Times Book Review*

'*Can't and Won't* is the most revolutionary collection of stories by an American in twenty-five years' John Freeman, *Boston Globe*

'Davis is wholly unique. A vast selection of tiny stories, some no more than a few lines long, all of them performing the alchemy of turning the everyday into quietly arresting, often wry, art' *Globe and Mail* (Canada)

'Short, shorter and brilliant: a unique and dazzling body of work' *Oregonian*

'Could a Lydia Davis story ever be mistaken for a story by someone else? You might as well ask if I could dream someone else's dream' *Book Forum*

'Inventive and rewarding' *Tatler*

'Strong and beguiling . . . *Can't and Won't* is evidence of a writer in total control of her own peculiar original voice . . . its pleasures are unexpected and manifold' *Elle* (US)

'Short stories aspire to the condition of poetry in this pithy and witty collection' *Independent*

'Even at her most poetic Davis is a storyteller, even if her plots unfold with the quiet philosophical precision of a Samuel Becket "fizzle" or theatrical monologue . . . when her genius for syntax is married to genuine emotion, then the results can be truly astonishing . . . touching, memorable, extraordinary' *Radar*

'Psychological richness and frequent poignancy . . . Davis hints insistently at how abundant nothingness can be when we bother to look at it' *The Times Literary Supplement*

'One of the strangest and most original writers in the English language . . . genuinely surprising. Astringent and penetrating, Davis's prose looks more than ever like one of the unique creations of American Literature' *Prospect*

ABOUT THE AUTHOR

Lydia Davis is the author of *Collected Stories*, one novel: *The End of the Story* and seven short-story collections, the most recent of which is *Can't and Won't*. She is the recipient of a MacArthur Fellowship and was named an Officer of the Order of Arts and Letters by the French government for her fiction and her translations of modern writers, including Gustave Flaubert and Marcel Proust. She won the Man Booker International Prize in 2013.

Can't and Won't

Lydia Davis

PENGUIN BOOKS

PENGUIN BOOKS

UK | USA | Canada | Ireland | Australia
India | New Zealand | South Africa

Penguin Books is part of the Penguin Random House group of companies
whose addresses can be found at global.penguinrandomhouse.com.

First published in the United States of America by Farrar, Strauss and Giroux 2014
First published in Great Britain by Hamish Hamilton 2014
Published in Penguin Books 2015
001

Printed in Great Britain by Clays Ltd, St Ives plc

A CIP catalogue record for this book is available from the British Library

ISBN: 978–0–241–96808–6

www.greenpenguin.co.uk

Penguin Random House is committed to a
sustainable future for our business, our readers
and our planet. This book is made from Forest
Stewardship Council® certified paper.

For Daniel and Theo
and for Laura and Stephanie

Contents

I

A Story of Stolen Salamis

My son's Italian landlord in Brooklyn kept a shed out back in which he cured and smoked salamis. One night, in the midst of a wave of petty vandalism and theft, the shed was broken into and the salamis were taken. My son talked to his landlord about it the next day, commiserating over the vanished sausages. The landlord was resigned and philosophical, but corrected him: "They were not sausages. They were salamis." Then the incident was written up in one of the city's more prominent magazines as an amusing and colorful urban incident. In the article, the reporter called the stolen goods "sausages." My son showed the article to his landlord, who hadn't known about it. The landlord was interested and pleased that the magazine had seen fit to report the incident, but he added: "They weren't sausages. They were salamis."

The Dog Hair

The dog is gone. We miss him. When the doorbell rings, no one barks. When we come home late, there is no one waiting for us. We still find his white hairs here and there around the house and on our clothes. We pick them up. We should throw them away. But they are all we have left of him. We don't throw them away. We have a wild hope—if only we collect enough of them, we will be able to put the dog back together again.

Circular Story

On Wednesday mornings early there is always a racket out there on the road. It wakes me up and I always wonder what it is. It is always the trash collection truck picking up the trash. The truck comes every Wednesday morning early. It always wakes me up. I always wonder what it is.

Idea for a Sign

At the start of a train trip, people search for a good seat, and some of them take a careful look at the people nearby who have already chosen their seats, to see if they will make good neighbors.

It might help if we each wore a little sign saying in what ways we will and will not be likely to disturb other passengers, such as: Will not talk on cell phone; will not eat smelly food.

Included in mine would be: Will not talk on cell phone at all, aside from perhaps a short communication to my husband at the beginning of the trip home, summarizing my visit in the city, or, more rarely, a quick warning to a friend on the way down that I will be late; but will recline my seat back as far as it will go, for most of the trip, except when I am eating my lunch or snack; may in fact be adjusting it slightly, back and up, from time to time throughout the trip; will sooner or later eat something, usually a sandwich, sometimes a salad or a container of rice pudding, actually two containers of rice pudding, though small ones; sandwich, almost always Swiss cheese, with in fact very little cheese, just a single slice, and lettuce and tomato, will not be noticeably smelly, at least as far as I can tell; am as tidy as I can be with the salad, but eating salad with a plastic fork is awkward and difficult; am tidy with the rice pudding, taking small bites, though when I remove the sealed top of the container it can make a loud ripping noise for just a moment; may keep unscrewing the top of my water bottle and taking a drink of water, especially while eating my sandwich and about one hour afterwards; may be more restless than some other passengers, and may clean my hands several times during the trip with a small bottle of hand sanitizer, sometimes using hand lotion afterwards, which involves reaching into my purse, taking out a small toiletries bag, unzipping it, and, when finished, zipping it up again and returning it to my purse; but may also sit perfectly quietly for a few minutes or longer staring out the window; may do nothing but read a book through most of the trip, except for one walk down the aisle to the restroom and back to my seat; but, on another day, may put the book down every few minutes, take a small notebook out of my purse, remove the rubber band from around it, and make a note in the notebook; or, when reading through a back issue of a literary magazine, may rip pages out in order to save them, though I will try to do this only when train is stopped at a station; lastly, after a day in the city, may untie my shoelaces and slip my shoes off for part of the trip, especially if the shoes are not very comfortable, then resting my bare feet on top of my shoes rather than directly on the floor, or, very rarely, may remove shoes and put on slippers, if I have a pair with me, keeping them on until I have nearly reached my destination; but feet are quite clean and toenails have a nice dark red polish on them.

Bloomington

Now that I have been here for a little while, I can say with confidence that I have never been here before.

The Cook's Lesson

story from Flaubert

Today I have learned a great lesson; our cook was my teacher. She is twenty-five years old and she's French. I discovered, when I asked her, that she *did not know* that Louis-Philippe is no longer king of France and we now have a republic. And yet it has been five years since he left the throne. She said the fact that he is no longer king simply does not interest her in the least—those were her words.

And I think of myself as an intelligent man! But compared to her I'm an imbecile.

At the Bank

I take my bag of pennies to the bank and throw them into a machine that will count them. I am asked by a teller to guess how much my pennies are worth. I guess $3.00. I am wrong. They amount to $4.24. But since I am within $1.99 of the correct sum, I qualify for a prize. Many people nearby in the bank congratulate me warmly. I may choose from among a number of prizes. When I refuse the first and the second, and seem likely to refuse the next, the anxious teller unlocks a secure vault and shows me the full array, which includes a large plastic piggy bank, a coloring book and crayons, and a small rubber ball. At last, so as not to disappoint her, I choose what I think is the best of them, a handsome Frisbee with its own carrying case.

dream

Awake in the Night

I can't go to sleep, in this hotel room in this strange city. It is very late, two in the morning, then three, then four. I am lying in the dark. What is the problem? Oh, maybe I am missing him, the person I sleep next to. Then I hear a door shut somewhere nearby. Another guest has come in, very late. Now I have the answer. I will go to his room and get in bed next to him, and then I will be able to sleep.

dream

At the Bank: 2

Again, I go to the bank with my bag full of pennies. Again, I guess that my pennies will add up to $3.00. The machine counts them. I have $4.92. Again, the bank teller decides that I am close enough to the correct amount to win a prize. I look forward to seeing what the selection of prizes will be this time, but there is only one prize—a tape measure. I am disappointed, but I accept it. At least this time I can see that the teller is a woman. Before, I could not be sure whether she was a woman or a man. But this time, though she is still bald, she moves more gracefully and smiles more gently, her voice is higher, and she is wearing a pin on her chest that says *Janet.*

dream

The Two Davises and the Rug

They were both named Davis, but they were not married to each other and they were not related by blood. They were neighbors, however. They were both indecisive people, or rather, they could be very decisive about some things, important things, or things to do with their work, but they could be very indecisive about smaller things, and change their minds from one day to the next, over and over again, being completely decided in favor of something one day and then completely decided against the same thing the next day.

They did not know this about each other until she decided to put her rug up for sale.

It was a brightly patterned wool rug, red, white, and black, with a bold design of diamonds and some black stripes. She had bought it at a Native American store near the town where she used to live, but now she found out it was not Native American. She had grown tired of it where it lay on the floor of her absent son's room, because it was a little dirty and curled up at the corners, and she decided to sell it in a group sale that was being held to raise money for a good cause. But when it was much admired at the sale, more than she expected, and when the price of ten dollars that she had put on it was raised by an appraiser to fifty dollars, she changed her mind and hoped that no one would buy it. As the day wore on, she did not lower the price on the rug, as others were lowering their prices around her, and though people continued to admire it, no one bought it.

The other Davis came to the sale early in the day and was immediately attracted to the rug. He hesitated, however, because the pattern was so bold and the colors so starkly red, white, and black that he thought it might not look good in his house, though his house was furnished in a clean, modern way. He admired the rug out loud to her, but told her he wasn't sure it would look right in his house and left the sale without buying it. During the day, however, while no one else was buying the rug and while she was not lowering the price, he was thinking about the rug, and later in the day he returned for the purpose of seeing the rug again, if it was still there, and making up his mind whether to buy it or not. The sale, however, had ended, all the goods had been either sold or bagged for donation, or packed up and taken back home, and the expanse of green lawn by the porch of the parish house, where the sale had been held, lay clear and smooth again in the late-afternoon shadows.

The other Davis was surprised and disappointed, and a day or two later, when he ran into this Davis at the post office, he said he had changed his mind about the rug and asked if it had been sold, and when she said it had not, he asked if he could try the rug in his house to see if it would look good.

This Davis was immediately embarrassed, because in the meantime she had decided she should keep the rug after all, clean it up, and try it out here and there in the house to see how it would look. But now, when the other Davis showed such interest in the rug, she was no longer sure she should do that. After all, she had been willing to sell it, and she had thought it was worth only ten dollars. She asked the other Davis if she could take a few more days to decide whether she was willing to part with it. The other Davis understood and said that was fine, to let him know if she decided she didn't want to keep the rug.

For a while she left it in her son's room, where it had originally been. She looked in on it now and then. It still looked a little dirty, with curled-up corners. She still found it somewhat attractive and at the same time somewhat unattractive. Then she thought she should bring it out where she would see it every day, so that she would feel more impelled to make a decision about whether or not to keep it. She knew the other Davis was waiting.

She put it on the landing between the first floor and the second floor, and thought it looked good with the drawing that hung on the wall there. But her husband thought it was too bright. She left it there, however, and continued to think about it whenever she went up or down the stairs. A day came when she decided quite firmly that although she found it quite attractive, the other Davis should have it, or at least try it out, because he liked it and it would probably look better in his house. But the next day, before she could act on her resolution, a friend came to the house and particularly admired the rug: this friend thought it was a new rug, and she thought it was very pretty. Now this Davis wondered if she shouldn't keep it after all.

Meanwhile, however, the days were passing, and she worried very much about the other Davis. She felt that he had clearly wanted to try the rug out and she was selfishly keeping it, even though she had been willing to sell it—and for only ten dollars. She felt that he probably wanted it, or admired it, more than she did. And yet she did not want to give up something that she had once admired enough to buy in the first place, and that other people also admired, and that she might like very much if she cleaned it up.

Now the rug entered her thoughts often, and she attempted to make up her mind about it almost daily, and changed her mind about it almost daily. She used different lines of reasoning to try and work out what she should do. The rug was a good one—an expert had told her that; she had bought it because she liked it in the Native American store, though apparently it was not Native American; her son liked it, the rare times he came home for a visit; she would still like it if it was cleaned up a little; but on the other hand, she had not kept it clean before and probably would not again; and the other Davis, to judge by the presentation of the interior of his house, which was clean and tidy and thoughtfully arranged, would clean it up and take good care of it; she had been ready to sell it; and the other Davis had been ready to buy it. The other Davis would probably be willing to pay the fifty dollars for it, which she would then give to the good cause. If she kept the rug, it occurred to her, she herself should probably give fifty dollars to the good cause, since she had been willing to sell it and no one had bought it—though then she would be paying fifty dollars to keep something that was already hers, unless perhaps it could no longer be considered really hers once it was put out for sale for the good cause.

One day she was given a large cardboard box full of fresh vegetables by the son of a friend: it was midsummer by now, and he had too many vegetables in his garden even to sell. There were too many vegetables in the box for her and her husband, and she decided to share them with some of her neighbors who did not have gardens. She gave some of the vegetables to a neighbor around the corner, a professional dancer who had recently moved into the neighborhood with his blind dog. When she left him, she took the rest of the vegetables across the street from him to the other Davis and his wife.

Now, as they were talking in the driveway about one thing and another, including the rug, she admitted to them that she often had a hard time making up her mind, and not only about the rug. Then the other Davis admitted that he, too, had a hard time making up his mind. His wife said it was amazing how firmly her husband could decide in favor of something, before he changed his mind and decided just as firmly against that thing. She said that it helped him to talk to her about whatever the thing was that he was trying to make up his mind about. She said her answers were usually, in sequence, over a period of time: "Yes, I think you're right"; "Do whatever you want"; "I don't care." She said that in this case, since both Davises were so indecisive, the rug was taking on a life of its own. She said they should give it a name. Both Davises liked that idea, but no name came to mind right away.

This Davis was left with the wish that there were a Solomon to turn to, for a judgment, because probably the question really was, not whether she did or didn't want to keep the rug, but, more generally, which of them really valued the rug more: she thought that if the other Davis valued it more than she did, he should have it; if she valued it more, she should keep it. Or perhaps the question had to be put a little differently, since it was, in a sense, already "her" rug: perhaps she merely had to decide that she valued it more than she had before, just enough more to keep it. But no, she thought again, if the other Davis really loved the rug more than she did, he should have it. She thought maybe she should suggest to the other Davis that he take it and keep it in his house for a while, to see whether he loved it very much, or merely liked it somewhat, or in fact did not want it at all. If he loved it, he should keep it; if he did not want it, she would keep it; if he merely liked it somewhat, she would keep it. But she was not sure this was the best solution, either.

Contingency (vs. Necessity)

He could be our dog.
But he is not our dog.
So he barks at us.

Brief Incident in Short *a*, Long *a*, and Schwa

Cat, gray tabby, calm, watches large black ant. Man, rapt, stands staring at cat and ant. Ant advances along path. Ant halts, baffled. Ant backtracks fast—straight at cat. Cat, alarmed, backs away. Man, standing, staring, laughs. Ant changes path again. Cat, calm again, watches again.

Contingency (vs. Necessity) 2: On Vacation

He could be my husband.
But he is not my husband.
He is her husband.
And so he takes her picture (not mine) as she stands in her flowered beach outfit in front of the old fortress.

A Story Told to Me by a Friend

A friend of mine told me a sad story the other day about a neighbor of hers. He had begun a correspondence with a stranger through an online dating service. The friend lived hundreds of miles away, in North Carolina. The two men exchanged messages and then photos and were soon having long conversations, at first in writing and then by phone. They found that they had many interests in common, were emotionally and intellectually compatible, were comfortable with each other, and were physically attracted to each other, as far as they could tell on the Internet. Their professional interests, too, were close, my friend's neighbor being an accountant and his new friend down South an assistant professor of economics at a small college. After some months, they seemed to be well and truly in love, and my friend's neighbor was convinced that "this was it," as he put it. When some vacation time came up, he arranged to fly down South for a few days and meet his Internet love.

During the day of travel, he called his friend two or three times and they talked. Then he was surprised to receive no answer. Nor was his friend at the airport to meet him. After waiting and calling several more times, my friend's neighbor left the airport and went to the address his friend had given him. No one answered when he knocked and rang. Every possibility went through his mind.

Here, some parts of the story are missing, but my friend told me that what her neighbor learned was that, on that very day, even as he was on his way south, his Internet friend had died of a heart attack while on the phone with his doctor; the traveler, having learned this either from the man's neighbor or from the police, had made his way to the local morgue; he had been allowed to view his Internet friend; and so it was here, face to face with a dead man, that he first laid eyes on the one who, he had been convinced, was to have been his companion for life.

The Bad Novel

This dull, difficult novel I have brought with me on my trip—I keep trying to read it. I have gone back to it so many times, each time dreading it and each time finding it no better than the last time, that by now it has become something of an old friend. My old friend the bad novel.

After You Left

story from Flaubert

You wanted me to tell you everything I did after we left each other.

Well, I was very sad; it had been so lovely. When I saw your back disappear into the train compartment, I went up on the bridge to watch your train pass under me. That was all I saw; you were inside it! I looked after it as long as I could, and I listened to it. In the other direction, towards Rouen, the sky was red and striped with broad bands of purple. The sky would be long dark by the time I reached Rouen and you reached Paris. I lit another cigar. For a while I paced back and forth. Then, because I felt so numb and tired, I went into a café across the street and drank a glass of kirsch.

My train came into the station, heading in the opposite direction from yours. In the compartment, I met a man I knew from my schooldays. We talked for a long time, almost all the way back to Rouen.

When I arrived, Louis was there to meet me, as we had planned, but my mother hadn't sent the carriage to take us home. We waited for a while, and then, by moonlight, we walked across the bridge and through the port. In that part of town there are two places where we could hire a hackney cab.

At the second place, the people live in an old church. It was dark. We knocked and woke the woman, who came to the door in her nightcap. Imagine the scene, in the middle of the night, with the interior of that old church behind her—her jaws gaping in a yawn; a candle burning; the lace shawl she wore hanging down below her hips. The horse had to be harnessed, of course. The breeching band had broken, and we waited while they mended it with a piece of rope.

On the way home, I told Louis about my old school friend, who is his old school friend, too. I told him how you and I had spent our time together. Out the window, the moon was shining on the river. I remembered another journey home late at night by moonlight. I described it to Louis: There was deep snow on the ground. I was in a sleigh, wearing my red wool hat and wrapped in my fur cloak. I had lost my boots that day, on my way to see an exhibition of savages from Africa. All the windows were open, and I was smoking my pipe. The river was dark. The trees were dark. The moon shone on the fields of snow: they looked as smooth as satin. The snow-covered houses looked like little white bears curled up asleep. I imagined that I was in the Russian steppe. I thought I could hear reindeer snorting in the mist, I thought I could see a pack of wolves leaping up at the back of the sleigh. The eyes of the wolves were shining like coals on both sides of the road.

When at last we reached home, it was one in the morning. I wanted to organize my work table before I went to bed. Out my study window, the moon was still shining—on the water, on the towpath, and, close to the house, on the tulip tree by my window. When I was done, Louis went off to his room and I went off to mine.

The Bodyguard

He goes with me wherever I go. He has fair hair. He is young and strong. His arms and legs are round and muscular. He is my bodyguard. But he never opens his eyes, and never leaves his armchair. Lying deep in the chair, he is carried from place to place, attended, in turn, by his own caregivers.

dream

The Child

She is bending over her child. She can't leave her. The child is laid out in state on a table. She wants to take one more photograph of the child, probably the last. In life, the child would never sit still for a photograph. She says to herself, "I'm going to get the camera," as if saying to the child, "Don't move."

dream

The Churchyard

I have the key to the churchyard and unlock the gate. The church is in the city, and it has a large enclosure. Now that the gate is open, many people come in and sit on the grass to enjoy the sun.

Meanwhile, girls at the street corner are raising money for their mother-in-law, who is called "La Bella."

I have offended or disappointed two women, but I am cradling Jesus (who is alive) amid a cozy pile of people.

dream

My Sister and the Queen
of England

For fifty years now, nag nag nag and harp harp harp. No matter what my sister did, it wasn't good enough for my mother, or for my father either. She moved to England to get away, and married an Englishman, and when he died, she married another Englishman, but that wasn't enough.

Then she was awarded the Order of the British Empire. My parents flew over to England and watched from across the ballroom floor as my sister walked out there alone and stood and talked to the Queen of England. They were impressed. My mother told me in a letter that no one else receiving honors that day talked to the Queen as long as my sister did. I wasn't surprised, because my sister has always been a great talker, no matter what the occasion. But when I asked my mother later what my sister was wearing, she didn't remember very well— white gloves and some kind of a tent, she said.

Four Lords of Parliament had mentioned my sister in their maiden speeches, because she had done so much for the disabled, and she treated the disabled, my mother said, like anyone else. She talked to her drivers the same way she talked to the Lords, and she talked to the Lords the same way she talked to the disabled. Everyone loved her, and no one minded that her house was a little untidy. My mother said the house was still untidy, and my sister was still letting her figure go, she invited too many people into her home, and she left the butter out all day, she told too much of her private business to her friend the Indian grocer on the corner, and she wouldn't stop talking, but my mother and father felt they had to keep quiet because how could they say anything against her now, she had done so much good and was so admired.

I'm proud of my sister, and I'm happy for her because of the award, but I'm also happy that my mother and father have finally been silenced for a while, and will let her alone for a while, though I don't think it will be for long, and I'm sorry it took the Queen of England to do it.

The Visit to the Dentist

story from Flaubert

Last week I went to the dentist, thinking he was going to pull my tooth. He said it would be better to wait and see if the pain subsided.

Well, the pain did not subside—I was in agony and running a fever. So yesterday I went to have it pulled. On my way to see him, I had to cross the old marketplace where they used to execute people, not so long ago. I remembered that when I was only six or seven years old, returning home from school one day, I crossed the square after an execution had taken place. The guillotine was there. I saw fresh blood on the paving stones. They were carrying away the basket.

Last night I thought about how I had entered the square on my way to the dentist dreading what was about to happen to me, and how, in the same way, those people condemned to death also used to enter that square dreading what was about to happen to them—though it was worse for them.

When I fell asleep, I dreamed about the guillotine; the strange thing was that my little niece, who sleeps downstairs, also dreamed about a guillotine, though I hadn't said anything to her about it. I wonder if thoughts are fluid, and flow downward, from one person to another, within the same house.

Letter to a Frozen Peas Manufacturer

Dear Frozen Peas Manufacturer,

We are writing to you because we feel that the peas illustrated on your package of frozen peas are a most unattractive color. We are referring to the 16 oz. plastic package that shows three or four pods, one of them split open, with peas rolling out near them. The peas are a dull yellow green, more the color of pea soup than fresh peas and nothing like the actual color of your peas, which are a nice bright dark green. The depicted peas are, moreover, about three times the size of the actual peas inside the package, which, together with their dull color, makes them even less appealing—they appear to be past their maturity and mealy in texture. Additionally, the color of your illustrated peas contrasts poorly with the color of the lettering and other decoration on your package, which is an almost harsh neon green. We have compared your depiction of peas to that of other frozen peas packages and yours is by far the least appealing. Most food manufacturers depict food on their packaging that is more attractive than the food inside and therefore deceptive. You are doing the opposite: you are falsely representing your peas as less attractive than they actually are. We enjoy your peas and do not want your business to suffer. Please reconsider your art.

Yours sincerely.

The Cornmeal

This morning, the bowl of hot cooked cornmeal, set under a transparent plate and left there, has covered the underside of the plate with droplets of condensation: it, too, is taking action in its own little way.

II

Two Undertakers

One undertaker, taking a body north on the highway, in France, stops at a roadside restaurant for a bite of lunch. There he meets another undertaker, a colleague known to him, who has also stopped for a bite of lunch and who is taking a body south. They decide to sit at the same table and have their meal together.

This encounter of two professionals is witnessed by Roland Barthes. It is his own deceased mother who is being taken south. He watches from a separate table, where he sits with his sister. His mother, of course, lies outside in the hearse.

I Ask Mary About Her Friend, the Depressive, and His Vacation

One year, she says
"He's away in the Badlands."

The next year, she says
"He's away in the Black Hills."

The Magic of the Train

We can see by the way they look from behind, as we watch them walk away from us down the train car, past the open doors of the toilets, through the sliding doors at the end, into some other part of the train, we can tell by the backs of them, these two women, in their tight black jeans, their platform heels, their tight sweaters and jean jackets in fashionable layers, their ample, loose, long black hair, the way they stride along, that they're in their late teens or maybe their early twenties. But when they come back the other way towards us, after a little while, from their excursion through the train to some strange and magical part of it up ahead, when they come back, still striding along, we can now see their faces, pale, haggard, with violet shadows under their eyes, sagging cheeks, odd moles here and there, laugh lines, crow's-feet, though they are both smiling a little, gently, and we see that in the meantime, under the magical effect of the train, they have aged twenty years.

Eating Fish Alone

Eating fish is something I generally do alone. I eat fish at home only when I am by myself in the house, because of the strong smell. I am alone with sardines on white bread with mayonnaise and lettuce, I am alone with smoked salmon on buttered rye bread, or tuna fish and anchovies in a salade Niçoise, or a canned salmon salad sandwich, or sometimes salmon cakes sautéed in butter.

I usually order fish, too, when I eat out. I order it because I like it and because it is not meat, which I rarely eat, or pasta, which is usually too rich, or a vegetarian dish, which I am likely to know all too well. I bring a book with me, though often the light over the table is not very good for reading and I am too distracted to read. I try to choose a table with good light, then I order a glass of wine and take out my book. I always want my glass of wine immediately, and I am very impatient until it comes. When it comes, and I have taken my first sip, I put my book down beside my plate and consider the menu, and my plan is always to order fish.

I love fish, but many fish should not be eaten anymore, and it has become difficult to know which fish I can eat. I carry with me in my wallet a little folding list put out by the Audubon Society that advises which fish to avoid, which fish to eat with caution, and which fish to eat freely. When I eat with other people I do not take this list out of my wallet, because it is not much fun to have dinner with someone who takes a list like this out of her wallet before she orders. I simply manage without it, though usually I can remember only that I should not eat farmed salmon or wild salmon, except for wild Alaskan salmon, which is never on the menu.

But when I am alone, I take out my list. No one will imagine, from a nearby table, that this list is what I am looking at. The trouble is, most kinds of fish on the restaurant menus are not fish one can eat freely. Some fish one cannot eat at all, ever, and other fish one may eat only if they come from the right place or are caught in the right way. I don't ask the waitress how the fish is caught, but I often ask where the fish is from. She usually does not know. This means that no one else has asked her that evening—either no one else is interested, or some are not interested and others know the answer already. If the waitress does not know the answer, she goes away to ask the chef, and then comes back with an answer, though it is usually not the one that I was hoping to hear.

I once asked a completely pointless question about halibut. I did not realize how pointless it was until the waitress had gone off to ask the chef. Pacific halibut is fine to eat, while Atlantic halibut is not. Even though I live on the Atlantic Coast, or near it, I asked her where the halibut was from, as though I had forgotten how far away the Pacific Ocean was, or as though halibut would be shipped all the way from the Pacific Coast to the Atlantic just for reasons of health or good fishing practices. As it happened, the restaurant was busy and she forgot to ask the chef, and by the time she returned I had realized that I should not order the halibut and was ready to order scallops instead. Scallops, my list said, were neither to be avoided nor to be eaten freely, but to be eaten with caution. I did not know what caution might mean in a restaurant situation, except perhaps that one should ask the waitress and the chef a few more questions than usual. But since even simple questions often did not produce very good answers, I did not expect good answers to detailed questions. Besides, I knew that the waitress and the chef did not have time for detailed questions. Certainly, if scallops were offered on the menu, the waitress or chef would not tell me they were endangered or unclean and advise me not to eat them. I ordered and ate them, and they were good, though I was a little uncomfortable, wondering whether they had been collected in the wrong way or contained toxic substances.

When I eat alone, I have no one to talk to and nothing to do but eat and drink, so my bites of food and my sips of wine are a little too deliberate. I keep thinking, It's time to take another bite, or Slow down, the food is almost gone, the meal will be over too soon. I try to read my book in order to make some time go by before I take another bite or another sip. But I can hardly understand what is on the page because I am reading so little at a time. I am also distracted by the other people in the room. I like to watch the waiters and waitresses and other customers very closely, even if they are not very interesting.

The fish on the restaurant menu are often not on my list. Turbot in champagne sauce was offered one night at a very good French restaurant near where I live, but it was not on my list. I might have had it, but I was told by the waiter that it was a very mild fish, so I thought it was probably not very tasty. Also, it came with a cheese crust on it. I said I thought the crust would be too rich. The waiter said it was a very thin crust. Even so, I decided against it. There were other fish on the menu: red snapper, which my list instructed me to avoid; Atlantic cod, which was endangered; and salmon, but not wild Alaskan salmon. I gave up on fish and ordered the restaurant's special plate of assorted vegetables, which arrived with small portions of many different vegetables, including fennel bulbs, arranged clockwise around a beautiful golden-brown molded potato cake. The different flavors of the vegetables were unexpectedly exciting, even though so many of them were root vegetables— not only carrots and potatoes, but also sautéed radishes, turnips, and parsnips.

The restaurant was owned by a couple from France. The wife greeted the guests and oversaw the service, and the husband cooked. As I left the restaurant that night, on my way to the parking lot I passed the windows of the kitchen. It was brightly lit and I stopped to look in. The chef was alone. He was dressed in white, wearing his chef's cap, and he was slim and active, bent over his chopping block. As far as I could see from that distance, his features were finely modeled and delicate, his expression intense. As I watched, he tipped his head back slightly and tossed a bit of food into his mouth, pausing to savor it. A younger man came in from the left carrying a tray of something, put it down, and went out again. He did not appear to have anything to do with the cooking. The chef was alone again. I had never before seen a real chef at work, and had never imagined that a chef would work alone in his kitchen. I could have watched him for a long time, but I felt it would be indiscreet to stay, and I walked away.

The last time I ate by myself, I was in a restaurant I chose because there was no alternative. I was far out in the country and it was the only one open. I thought it would not be very good. It had a loud, popular bar in the front. I ordered a beer this time, and looked at the menu. The fish special was a marlin steak. I tried to think what marlin was. I had not thought of marlin for a long time. Then I pictured the fish sailing through the air with a large fin on its back, and I was almost sure it was popular for sport fishing, but I could not imagine what it tasted like. It was not on my list, but I ordered it anyway. Since I did not know whether I should avoid it, there was a chance that it was all right. Even if it wasn't all right, of course, I could still occasionally have a fish that I should not have.

When she brought the fish, the waitress passed along a message from the chef: he would be waiting to know how I liked it; it was such a beautiful steak, he said. I was impressed by his enthusiasm, and as I ate, I paid more careful attention than usual. The chef had time to be interested in this marlin steak, I suppose, because it was a Monday night and only one other table was occupied in the large dining room, though as I ate my meal, a few more people came in. Even the bar had only two customers, small old men in plaid flannel shirts. But with the loud television and the laughter of the barmaid, who was also the hostess and the wife of the chef, the bar was still noisy.

The marlin was good, if a little chewy. When the waitress came by to see how I liked it, I did not tell her it was chewy. I told her it was very good, and that I liked the delicacy of the herbs in the sauce. At one point in the meal, as I continued eating slowly, this time without reading, the chef emerged from the kitchen in the distance. He was a tall man with a slight stoop to his shoulders. He walked over to the bar to have a drink and say a few words to his wife and the old men, and then walked back. Before he pushed through the swinging door, he turned a moment to look across the dining room in my direction, curious, I'm sure, to know who was eating his beautiful marlin steak. I looked back at him. I would have waved, but before I thought of it he disappeared through the door.

The serving of food on my plate, the marlin steak and baked potato and vegetables, was generous, and I could not eat all of it. I ate all the vegetables, at least, tender slices of lightly sautéed zucchini with thin strips of red pepper and herbs, and asked the waitress if she would wrap up the rest for me to take home. She was worried; I had eaten only half the fish. "But you did like it?" she asked. She was young. I thought she was the daughter of the chef and the barmaid. I assured her I had. Now I was worried; the chef might not believe I had truly liked the fish, though I had. There was nothing more I could say about it, but as I paid my bill, I told the waitress I had loved the vegetables. "Most people don't eat them," she said matter-of-factly. I thought of the waste, and the care with which the chef prepared, over and over again, the vegetables that no one ate. At least I had eaten his vegetables, and he would know that I had liked them. But I was sorry I had not eaten all of his marlin. I could have done that.

Can't and Won't

I was recently denied a writing prize because, they said, I was *lazy*. What they meant by *lazy* was that I used too many contractions: for instance, I would not write out in full the words *cannot* and *will not*, but instead contracted them to *can't* and *won't*.

Pouchet's Wife

story from Flaubert

Tomorrow I will be going into Rouen for a funeral. Madame Pouchet, the wife of a doctor, died the day before yesterday in the street. She was on horseback, riding with her husband; she had a stroke and fell from the horse. I've been told I don't have much compassion for other people, but in this case, I am very sad. Pouchet is a good man, though completely deaf and by nature not very cheerful. He doesn't see patients, but works in zoology. His wife was a pretty Englishwoman with a pleasant manner who helped him a good deal in his work. She made drawings for him and read his proofs; they went on trips together; she was a real *companion*. He loved her very much and will be devastated by his loss. Louis lives across the street from them. He happened to see the carriage that brought her home, and her son lifting her out; there was a handkerchief over her face. Just as she was being carried like that into the house, feet first, an errand boy came up. He was delivering a large bouquet of flowers she had ordered that morning. O Shakespeare!

Dinner

I am still in bed when friends of ours arrive at the house for dinner. My bed is in the kitchen. I get up to see what I can make for them. I find three or four packages of hamburger in the refrigerator, some partly used and some untouched. I think I can put all the hamburger together and make a meatloaf. This would take an hour, but nothing else occurs to me. I go back to bed for a while to think about it.

dream

The Dog

We are about to leave a place that has a large flower garden and a fountain. I look out the car window and see our dog lying on a gurney in the doorway of a sort of shed. His back is to us. He is lying still. There are two cut flowers placed on his neck, one red and one white. I look away and then back—I want to see him one last time. But the doorway of the shed is empty. In that one moment he has vanished: a moment too soon, they have wheeled him away.

dream

The Grandmother

A person has come to my house carrying a large peach tart. He has also brought with him some other people, including an old woman who complains about the gravel and is then carried into the house with great difficulty. At the table, she observes to one man, by way of conversation, that she likes his teeth. Another man keeps shouting in her face, but she is not frightened, she only looks at him balefully. Later, at home, it is discovered that while she was eating cashews from a bowl, she also ate her hearing aid. Even though she chewed on it for nearly two hours, she could not reduce it to particles small enough to swallow. At bedtime she spat it out into the hand of her caregiver and told him this nut was a bad one.

dream

The Dreadful Mucamas

They are very rigid, stubborn women from Bolivia. They resist and sabotage whenever possible.

They came with the apartment which we are subletting. They were bargains because of Adela's low IQ. She is a scatterbrain.

In the beginning, I said to them: *I'm very happy that you can stay, and I am sure that we will get along very well.*

This is an example of the problems we are having. It is a typical incident that has just taken place. I needed to cut a piece of thread and could not find my six-inch scissors. I accosted Adela and told her I could not find my scissors. She protested that she had not seen them. I went with her to the kitchen and asked Luisa if she would cut my thread. She asked me why I did not simply bite it off. I said I could not thread my needle if I bit it off. I asked her please to get some scissors and cut it off—now. She told Adela to look for the scissors of la Señora Brodie, and I followed her to the study to see where they were kept. She removed them from a box. At the same time I saw a long, untidy piece of twine attached to the box and asked her why she did not trim off the frayed end of it while she had the scissors. She shouted that it was impossible. The twine might be needed to tie up the box some time. I admit that I laughed. Then I took the scissors from her and cut it off myself. Adela shrieked.

Her mother appeared behind her. I laughed again and now they both shrieked. Then they were quiet.

I have told them: *Please, do not make the toast until we ask for breakfast. We do not like very crisp toast the way the English do.*

I have told them: *Every morning, when I ring the bell, please bring us our mineral water immediately. Afterwards, make the toast and at the same time prepare fresh coffee with milk. We prefer Franja Blanca or Cinta Azul coffee from Bonafide.*

I spoke pleasantly to Luisa when she came with the mineral water before breakfast. But when I reminded her about the toast, she broke into a tirade—how could I think she would ever let the toast get cold or hard? But it is almost always cold and hard.

We have told them: *We prefer that you always buy Las Tres Niñas or Germa milk from Kasdorf.*

Adela cannot speak without yelling. I have asked her to speak gently, and to say "Señora," but she never does. They also speak very loudly to each other in the kitchen.

Often, before I have said three words to Adela, she yells at me: *Si . . . si, si, si . . . !* and leaves the room. I honestly don't think I can stand it.

•

I say to Luisa: *Don't interrupt me!* I say: *No me interrumpe!*

The problem is not that Adela does not work hard enough. But she comes to my room with a message from her mother: she tells me the meal I have asked for is impossible, and she shakes her finger back and forth, screaming at the top of her voice.

They are both, mother and daughter, such willful, brutal women. At times I think they are complete barbarians.

I have told Adela: *If necessary, clean the hall, but do not use the vacuum cleaner more than twice a week.*
    Last week she refused point-blank to take the vacuum cleaner out of the front hall by the entrance—just when we were expecting a visit from the Rector of Patagonia.

They have such a sense of privilege and ownership.

I have asked them: *First listen to what I have to say!*

I took my underthings out to them to be washed. Luisa immediately said that it was too hard to wash a girdle by hand. I disagreed, but I did not argue.

Adela refuses to do any work in the morning but housecleaning.

•

I say to them: *We are a small family. We do not have any children.*

When I go to them to inquire about the tasks I have given them, I find they are usually engaged in their own occupations—washing their sweaters or telephoning.

The ironing is never done on time.

Today I reminded them both that my underthings needed to be washed. They did not respond. Finally I had to wash my slip myself.

I say to them: *We have noticed that you have tried to improve, and in particular that you are doing our washing more quickly now.*

I have asked Adela: *Please, do not leave the dirt and the cleaning things in the hall.*

I have asked her: *Please, collect the trash and take it to the incinerator immediately.*

Today I told Adela that I needed her there in the kitchen, but she went to her mother's room and came back with her sweater on and went out anyway. She was buying some lettuce—for them, it turned out, not for us.

At each meal, she makes an effort to escape.

As I was passing through the dining room this morning, I tried, as usual, to chat pleasantly with Adela. Before I could say two words, however, she retorted sharply that she could not do anything else while she was setting the table.

Adela rushes out of the kitchen into the living room even when guests are present and shouts: *Telephone for you in your room!*

Although I have asked her to speak gently, she never does. Today she came rushing out of the kitchen into the dining room saying: *Telephone, for you!* and pointed at me. Later she did the same with our luncheon guest, a professor.

I say to Luisa: *I would like to discuss the program for the days to come. Today I do not need more than a sandwich at noon, and fruit. But el señor would like a nutritious tea.*

Tomorrow we would like a rather nourishing tea with hard-boiled eggs and sardines at six, and we will not want any other meal at home.

At least once a day, we want to eat cooked vegetables. We like salads, but we also like cooked vegetables. Sometimes we could eat both salad and cooked vegetables at the same meal.

We do not have to eat meat at lunchtime, except on special occasions. We are very fond of omelets, perhaps with cheese or tomato.

Please serve our baked potatoes immediately after taking them from the oven.

We had had nothing but fruit at the end of the meal for two weeks. I asked Luisa for a dessert. She brought me some little crepes filled with applesauce. They were nice, though quite cold. Today she gave us fruit again.

•

I said to her: *Luisa, you cannot refer to my instructions as "capricious and illogical."*

Luisa is emotional and primitive. Her moods change rapidly. She readily feels insulted and can be violent. She has such pride.

Adela is simply wild and rough, a harebrained savage.

I say to Luisa: *Our guest, Señor Flanders, has never visited the park. He would like to spend several hours there. Can you make sandwiches of cold meat for him to take with him? It is his last Sunday here.*

For once, she does not protest.

When setting the dining table, Adela puts each thing down with a bang.

I say to Luisa: *Please, I would like Adela to polish the candlesticks. We are going to have them on the table at night.*

I ring the bell at the dining table, and a loud crash follows instantly in the kitchen.

I have told them: *There should not be these kitchen noises during our cocktail and dinner hour.* But they are hitting each other again and yelling.

If we ask for something during a meal, Adela comes out of the kitchen and says: *There isn't any.*

It is all so very nerve-racking. I often feel worn out after just one attempt to speak to her.

Luisa, I say, I want to make sure we understand each other. You cannot play the radio in the kitchen during our dinnertime. There is also a lot of shouting in the kitchen. We are asking for some peace in the house.

We do not believe they are sincerely trying to please us.

Adela sometimes takes the bell off the dining table and does not put it back on. Then I cannot ring for her during the meal but have to call loudly from the dining room to the kitchen, or go without what I need, or get the bell myself so that I can ring it. My question is: Does she leave the bell off the table on purpose?

I instruct them ahead of time: *For the party we will need tomato juice, orange juice, and Coca-Cola.*

I tell her: *Adela, you will be the one in charge of answering the door and taking the coats. You will show the ladies where the toilet is, if they ask you.*

I ask Luisa: *Do you know how to prepare empanadas in the Bolivian style?*

We would like them both to wear uniforms *all* the time.

I say to Adela: *Please, I would like you to pass among the guests frequently with plates of hors d'oeuvres that have been recently prepared.*
    When the plates no longer look attractive, please take them back out to the kitchen and prepare fresh ones.
    I say to her: *Please, Adela, I would like there always to be clean glasses on the table, and also ice and soda.*
    I have told her: *Always leave a towel on the rack above the bidet.*

I say to her: *Are there enough vases? Can you show them to me? I would like to buy some flowers.*

Here are more of the details of the silent warfare: I see that Adela has left a long string lying on the floor next to the bed. She has gone away with the wastebasket. I don't know if she is testing me. Does she think I am too meek or ignorant to require her to pick it up? But she has a cold, and she isn't very bright, and if she really did not notice the string, I don't want to make too much of it. I finally decide to pick up the string myself.

We suffer from their rude and ruthless vengeance.

A button was missing from my husband's shirt collar. I took the shirt to Adela. She shook her finger and said no. She said that la Señora Brodie always took everything to the dressmaker to be mended.

Even a button? I asked. Were there no buttons in the house? She said there were no buttons in the house.

I told Luisa they could go out on Sundays, even before breakfast. She yelled at me that they did not want to go out, and asked me, Where would they go?

I said that they were welcome to go out, but that if they did not go out, we would expect them to serve us something, even if it was something simple. She said she would, in the morning, but not in the afternoon. She said that her two older daughters always came to see her on Sundays.

I spent the morning writing Luisa a long letter, but I decided not to give it to her.

In the letter I told her: *I have employed many maids in my life*.

I told her that I believe I am a considerate, generous, and fair employer.

I told her that when she accepts the realities of the situation, I'm sure everything will go well.

If only they would make a real change in their attitude, we would like to help them. We would pay to have Adela's teeth repaired, for instance. She is so ashamed of her teeth.

But up to now there has been no real change in their attitude.

We also think they may have relatives living secretly with them behind the kitchen.

I am learning and practicing a sentence that I will try on Luisa, though it may sound more hopeful than I feel: *Con el correr del tiempo, todo se solucionará.*

But they give us such dark, Indian looks!

Reversible Story

NECESSARY EXPENDITURE

A concrete mixer has come and gone from the house next door. Mr. and Mrs. Charray are renovating their wine cellar. If they improve their cellar, they will pay less for fire insurance. At the moment, their fire insurance is very expensive. The reason for this is that they own thousands of bottles of very good wine. They have very good wine and some fine paintings, but their taste in clothes and furniture is strictly lower middle class.

EXPENDITURE NECESSARY

The Charrays' taste in clothes and furniture is dull and strictly lower middle class. However, they do own some fine paintings, many by contemporary Canadian and American painters. They also have some good wine. In fact, they own thousands of bottles of very good wine. Because of this, their fire insurance is very expensive. But if they enlarge and otherwise improve their wine cellar, the fire insurance will be less expensive. They are doing this: a concrete mixer has just come and gone from their house, next door.

A Woman, Thirty

A woman, thirty, does not want to leave her childhood home.

Why should I leave home? These are my parents. They love me. Why should I go marry some man who will argue and shout at me?

Still, the woman likes to undress in front of the window. She wishes some man would at least look at her.

How I Know What I Like
(Six Versions)

She likes it. She is like me. Therefore, I might like it.

She is like me. She likes the things I like. She likes this. So I might like it.

I like it. I show it to her. She likes it. She is like me. Therefore, I might really like it.

I think I like it. I show it to her. She likes it. She is like me. Therefore, I might really like it.

I think I like it. I show it to her. (She is like me. She likes the things I like.) She likes it. So I might really like it.

I like it. I show it to her. She likes it. (She says the other one is "just plain awful.") She is like me. She likes the things I like. So I might really like it.

Handel

I have a problem in my marriage, which is that I simply do not like George Frideric Handel as much as my husband does. It is a real barrier between us. I am envious of one couple we know, for example, who both love Handel so much they will sometimes fly all the way to Texas just to hear a particular tenor sing a part in one of his operas. By now, they have also converted another friend of ours into a lover of Handel. I am surprised, because the last time she and I talked about music, what she loved was Hank Williams. All three of them went by train to Washington, D.C., this year to hear *Giulio Cesare in Egitto*. I prefer the composers of the nineteenth century and particularly Dvořák. But I'm pretty open to all sorts of music, and usually if I'm exposed to something long enough, I come to like it. But even though my husband puts on some sort of Handel vocal music almost every night if I don't say anything to stop him, I have not come to love Handel. Fortunately, I have just found out that there is a therapist not too far from here, in Lenox, Massachusetts, who specializes in Handel-therapy, and I'm going to give her a try. (My husband does not believe in therapy and I know he would not go to a Dvořák-therapist with me even if there was one.)

The Force of the Subliminal

Rhea was here for an overnight visit and we were talking about birthdays. I had asked her when her birthday was. She told me it was April 13, but that she never received any cards or gifts on her birthday, which was just as well because she did not want to be reminded of it. I remarked that one person who never let anyone forget her birthday was our mutual friend Ellie.

Ellie was far away, in another country, where it was harder for her to remind people of her birthday. Then I thought, Why, it's October: this is the month of Ellie's birthday! I could not remember which day in October it was, so I went and looked it up where I had written it down in my address book. I discovered it was this very day, October 23. I told Rhea and we exclaimed over the fact that I had started talking about birthdays on Ellie's birthday. Rhea said I must have known it all along, subliminally.

I did not tell Rhea how I had come to think of birthdays: that as I was putting napkins on the table for dinner I remembered a story she had told me, how she was once, long ago, giving dinner to a group of our friends who were rather difficult to entertain since their standards were very high where food and wine and table service were concerned; how Rhea, who in those days did not usually care much about such things as table settings, but was capable of embarrassment in the presence of certain people such as these friends, discovered first that she had no napkins of any kind in the house, then no paper towels either, then no Kleenex tissues either; and how, a few minutes into the meal, one of the guests politely asked for a napkin; how Rhea explained the problem and another guest suggested using toilet paper; and Rhea's embarrassment as the guests did continue the meal using toilet paper; so that I was moved to want to send Rhea a set of cloth napkins for her next birthday so that she would never find herself in that situation again. But it was true that I might not have thought of Rhea's story if I had not remembered, subliminally, that today was Ellie's birthday.

Later, after Rhea had gone to bed, while I was washing the last of the dinner dishes, I thought about the conversation and said to myself, with a feeling of mild satisfaction, Well, this is one year that Ellie has not been able to remind me of her birthday, because she is too far away. But then I thought, Wait a minute, the fact is that I have somehow remembered Ellie's birthday. And then I realized that because she never lets anyone forget her birthday, and because I know this so well, it was not I who had subliminally known it all along, as Rhea and I had decided, but in fact Ellie who had managed, in the end, to remind me, though not as directly as usual, and also, with her characteristic efficiency, to remind Rhea at the same time.

Her Geography: Alabama

She thinks, for a moment, that Alabama is a city in Georgia: it is called Alabama, Georgia.

The Funeral

story from Flaubert

I went to Pouchet's wife's funeral yesterday. As I watched poor Pouchet, who stood there bending and swaying with grief like a stalk of grass in the wind, some fellows near me began talking about their orchards: they were comparing the girths of the young fruit trees. Then a man next to me asked me about the Middle East. He wanted to know whether there were any museums in Egypt. He asked me: "What is the condition of their public libraries?" The priest standing over the hole was speaking French, not Latin, because the service was a Protestant one. The gentleman beside me approved, then made some slighting remarks about Catholicism. Meanwhile, there was poor Pouchet standing forlornly in front of us.

Oh, we writers may think we invent too much—but reality is worse every time!

The Husband-Seekers

Flocks of women attempt to land on an island, seeking husbands from a tribe of very beautiful young men. They blow across the sea like cotton buds or seeding wild plants, and when rejected they pile up offshore in a floating bank of woolly white.

dream

In the Gallery

A woman I know, a visual artist, is trying to hang her work for a show. Her work is a single line of text pasted on the wall, with a transparent curtain suspended in front of it.

She is at the top of a ladder and cannot get down. She is facing out instead of in. The people down below tell her to turn around, but she does not know how.

When I see her again, she is down from the ladder. She is going from one person to the next, asking for help in hanging her artwork. But no one will help her. They say she is such a difficult woman.

dream

The Low Sun

I am a college girl. I tell a younger college girl, a dancer, that the sun is very low in the sky now. Its light must be filling the caves by the sea.

dream

The Landing

Just now, during these days when I am so afraid of dying, I have been through a strange experience on an airplane.

I was on my way to Chicago to take part in a conference. The emergency occurred as we were approaching the airport. This is something I have always dreaded. Each time I fly in an airplane, I try to make my peace with the world and gain some final perspective on my life. I always do this twice on the flight, once before takeoff and once before landing. But there has never before been anything worse, on any of these flights, than ordinary turbulence—although of course when the turbulence begins, I don't know that it will be nothing more than ordinary turbulence.

This time something was wrong with the wings. Some flaps were not opening that were supposed to slow the plane down as it approached the runway, so it was going to have to land at a very high speed. There was a danger that when it landed, going at such a high speed, a tire could burst and the plane might spin and crash, or the wheels could collapse and the plane might slide on its belly and catch fire.

The announcement, from the pilot, terrified me. The terror was very physical, something like an icy bolt down my spine. With his announcement, everything had changed: we might all die within the next hour. I looked, for comfort or companionship in my fear, at the woman in the seat next to me, but she was no help, her eyes closed and her face turned away towards the window. I looked at other passengers, but each seemed absorbed in comprehending what the pilot had said. I, too, shut my eyes, and held on to the arms of my seat.

A little time passed, and then there was a clarification from the steward, who announced approximately how long we would be circling above the airport. The steward was calm. As he spoke, I kept my eyes fixed on his face. This was when I learned something I stored away to remember later, on other flights, if there were to be other flights: if I was worried, I should look at the face of the steward or stewardess and read his or her expression for a clue as to whether I should be worried or not. This steward's face was smooth and relaxed. The emergency was not one of the worst, he added. I looked across the aisle and met the eyes of a passenger in his sixties who was also calm. He told me he had flown over nine million miles since 1981 and experienced a number of emergency situations. He did not go on to describe them.

But now the steward was doing something that only intensified my fear: still calm, but perhaps with the calm of fatalism, I now thought, fatalism produced by his long training and experience, or perhaps simply an acceptance of the end, he was instructing the people in the first row point by point what each of them was to do in case he himself became incapacitated. Watching him instruct them, in my eyes they were suddenly elevated from being mere passengers to being his assistants or deputies, and I saw him, already, reduced to helplessness, dead or paralyzed. Even if only in my imagination, the fatal crash was already imminent. At that point, I realized that anything other than routine behavior from a steward or stewardess would alarm me.

Our lives might be almost over. This required an immediate reconciliation with the idea of death, and it required an immediate decision as to the best way to leave this world. What should be my last thoughts on this earth, in this life? It was not a matter of looking for solace but for acceptance, some way of believing that it was all right to die now. First I said goodbye to certain people close to me. Then I had to have a larger thought, for the very end, and what I found to be the best thought was the thought that I was very small in this large universe. It was necessary to picture the large universe, and all the galaxies, and remember how very small I was, and then it would be all right that I should die now. Things were dying all the time, the universe was mysterious, another ice age was coming anyway, our civilization would disappear, so it was all right that I should die now.

While I was thinking this large thought, my eyes were again shut, I was clasping my hands together until they were moist, and I was bracing my feet very hard against the base of the seat in front of me. It wouldn't help to brace my feet if we had a fatal crash. But I had to take what little action I could, I had to assert my tiny amount of control. In the midst of my fear, I still found it interesting that I thought I had to assert some control in an uncontrollable situation. Then I gave up taking any action at all and observed another interesting thing about what was happening now inside me—that as long as I felt I had to take some action, I was anguished, and when I gave up all responsibility and stopped trying to do anything at all, I was relatively at peace, even though the earth meanwhile was circling so far below us and we were so high up in a defective airplane that would have trouble landing.

The airplane circled for a long time. Either later, or at the time, I learned that while we were circling, preparations were being made on the ground for an emergency landing. The longest runway was being cleared, because the plane would be coming in at a high speed and would therefore have to travel a long way as it slowed down. Fire engines were brought out and parked by the runway. There were several possible problems with landing at such a high speed. The wheels could give way and collapse, the plane then coasting on its belly. The friction of coasting could cause a fire, or the speed of the plane could cause it to tip forward, crushing its nose. If the plane was coasting on its belly, or if a tire burst, the pilot could lose control of the steering and the plane could veer off the runway and crash.

At last the long runway was clear and the fire engines were in place, and the pilot began the descent. We passengers could not perceive anything out of the ordinary in the way he was flying the plane during the descent, but as the moment came for landing we grew more nervous: whereas before, the possible disaster was in our near future and we were still untouched, now it was just moments away.

In a normal landing, a plane comes in quite steeply, maybe at a 30-degree angle, and it often then bumps or bounces a little on the ground as it makes contact. Moving at such a high speed, we could not safely do that, so the pilot descended in wide circles almost all the way down to the ground before he headed for the runway, approaching it so low that its path was at almost no angle to the ground. In order to have the whole length of the runway for decelerating, he touched the plane down as soon as he passed the edge of the runway, putting the wheels to the asphalt so gently that we hardly felt it: the landing was smoother than any I had experienced before. He then slowed the plane very gradually until we were taxiing at a normal speed. He had done a beautiful job of landing, and we were safe.

Now, of course, the passengers all clapped and roared, in their relief, at the same time looking at one another and gazing out the windows in some awe at the fire engines that had not been needed. As the cheering died down, the sound of talking and laughing in the cabin increased. The man across the aisle told me about other near-disasters he had experienced, such as a fire aboard his airplane. We were informed by the steward, who also became more talkative now that we were on the ground, that pilots practice this sort of landing many times in their training. It might have helped us to know this earlier, but perhaps it would not have.

I was thinking about the landing over my dinner that night, in the orderly, bustling ground-floor restaurant of my hotel. I was looking into the face of a very small fried egg, a quail egg, on my plate, and it occurred to me that if the outcome had been different, the egg would at this very moment still have been looking up at someone, but at someone else, not me. The egg would have been looking up at a different fork, or even the same fork, but in a different hand. My hand would have been somewhere else, maybe in a Chicago morgue.

I was also writing down what I could remember of the landing, while my dinner cooled. The waiter, observing my plate, said something like "Your pen is moving faster than your fork," and then he added, as an afterthought, "which is the way it should be." At that, I liked him better. I had not liked him before, with his lank locks of hair and his overly friendly jokes.

Meanwhile, in the background, at the hotel reception desk, a slim, cautious, gray-bearded Englishman was asked by the clerk, "What is your name?" and he answered, "Morris. M, o, r, r, i, s."

The Language of the
Telephone Company

"The trouble you reported recently
is now working properly."

The Coachman and the Worm

story from Flaubert

A former servant of ours, a pathetic fellow, is now the driver of a hackney cab—you'll probably remember how he married the daughter of that porter who was awarded a prestigious prize at the same time that his wife was being sentenced to penal servitude for theft, whereas he, the porter, was actually the thief. In any case, this unfortunate man, Tolet, our former servant, has, or thinks he has, a tapeworm inside him. He talks about it as though it were a living person who communicates with him and tells him what it wants, and when Tolet is talking to you, the word "he" always refers to this creature inside him. Sometimes Tolet has a sudden urge and attributes it to the tapeworm: "*He* wants it," he says— and right away Tolet obeys. Lately *he* wanted to eat some fresh white rolls; another time *he* had to have some white wine, but the next day *he* was outraged because he wasn't given red.

The poor man has by now lowered himself, in his own eyes, to the same level as the tapeworm; they are equals waging a fierce battle for dominance. He said to my sister-in-law recently, "That creature has it in for me; it's a battle of wills, you see; he's forcing me to do what he likes. But I'll have my revenge. Only one of us will be left alive." Well, the man is the one who will be left alive, or, rather, not for long, because, *in order to kill the worm and be rid of it*, he recently swallowed a *bottle of vitriol* and is at this very moment dying. I wonder if you can see the true depths of this story.

What a strange thing it is—the human brain!

Letter to a Marketing Manager

Dear Harvard Book Store Marketing Manager,

I recently telephoned your bookstore to inquire about the matter described below and was told that you would be the person to contact. My question concerns an unfortunate biographical mistake printed in your January 2002 newsletter.

I was startled to see, on the back page of this issue, that my recently published book was featured in the column titled "Spotlight: McLean Alumni." Now, I am aware that McLean's has a distinguished list of former patients and is among the most prestigious of institutions of this type in the country, but I have been inside its walls only once, and that was as a visitor. I stopped in to see a friend of mine from high school, and spent no more than, perhaps, one awkward hour with him, since our conversation was at best difficult.

Now, to be perfectly honest—in case this is the source of the misunderstanding—it is true that a member of my family was once incarcerated in McLean's. My great-grandfather, of the same surname, was for a time a patient of the institution, but this was in the early part of the last century, and he was not a seriously disturbed individual, as far as I can tell from what my father has said and from the letters and other documentary evidence I have in my possession. He was apparently no more than generally restless, apathetic at his place of employment, occasionally inspired with plans for irrational enterprises, dissatisfied with domestic life, and visibly oppressed by his wife's emphatically demanding and restrictive nature. Although he did indeed escape the institution once and was then forcibly returned to it, he was several months later judged to have been rehabilitated, and he was released. He thereafter lived a tranquil, if rather solitary, life apart from his family, with a single manservant, on a farm in Harwich, Massachusetts.

I offer this information in case it may be useful, though I can think of no reason why you would confuse me with him. However, no other explanation occurs to me for your mistaken identification, unless your buyers assumed on the basis of the contents of my book, its title, or my admittedly somewhat wild-eyed photograph that at some time in the past I was an inmate of McLean's.

It is always nice to have some attention paid to one's book, but embarrassing to be misidentified in this way. Could you please throw some light on the matter?

Yours sincerely.

III

The Last of the Mohicans

We are sitting with our old mother in the nursing home.

"Of course I'm lonesome for you kids. But it's not like being in a strange place, where you don't know anyone."

She smiles, trying to reassure us. "There are plenty of people here from good old Willy."

She adds: "Of course, a lot of them can't talk." She pauses, and goes on: "A lot of them can't see."

She looks at us through her thick-lensed glasses. We know she can't see anything but light and shadow.

"I'm the last of the Mohicans—as they say."

Grade Two Assignment

Color these fish.
Cut them out.
Punch a hole in the top of each fish.
Put a ribbon through all the holes.
Tie these fish together.

Now read what is written on these fish:
Jesus is a friend.
Jesus gathers friends.
I am a friend of Jesus.

Master

"You want to be a master," he said. "Well, you're not a master."

That took me down a peg.

Seems I still have a lot to learn.

An Awkward Situation

A young writer has hired an older, more experienced writer to improve upon his texts. However, he refuses to pay her. He keeps her, in fact, in a situation that amounts to imprisonment, on the grounds of his estate. Though his frail and elderly mother, while turning her back and walking away, as though unwilling to look at him, urges him, weakly, to pay this writer what he owes her, he does not. Instead, he holds his arm out straight towards her, his hand in a fist, while she holds her hand out under his fist, palm up, as though to receive something. He then opens his hand, and it is empty. He is doing this for revenge, she knows, because he and she were once involved in what might be called a love relationship, and she was not as kind to him as she should have been. She was sometimes rude to him, and belittled him, both in front of others and in private. She tries, over and over, to think whether she was as cruel to him then, so long ago, as he is being cruel to her now. Complicating the situation is the fact that another person is living here with her, and depending on her for support, and that is her ex-husband. He, unlike her, and unlike her bitter former lover, is cheerful and confident, not knowing, until at last she tells him, that she is not being paid. Even then, however, after a moment's pause in which he absorbs the news, he continues to be cheerful and confident, in part, perhaps, because he does not believe her, and in part because he is distracted, having just embarked on another writing project of his own. He invites her to work with him on it. She is interested and willing, until she looks at it. She then sees that, unfortunately for her, it involves the writing of yet another person. She does not like the writing, or the character, or what she suspects is the corrupting influence, of this other person, and she does not want to be associated with her. But before she can tell him this, or, better, hide it from him, while still declining to collaborate on the writing project, another question occurs to her. Where, in all this, she wonders now, after a surprisingly long time, perhaps weeks, is her own present husband, always so helpful to her, and why does he not come to help her out of this most awkward situation?

Housekeeping Observation

Under all this dirt
the floor is really very clean.

The Execution

story from Flaubert

Here is another story about our compassion. In a village not far from here, a young man murdered a banker and his wife, then raped the servant girl and drank all the wine in the cellar. He was tried, found guilty, sentenced to death, and executed. Well, there was such interest in seeing this peculiar fellow die on the guillotine that people came from all over the country-side the night before—more than *ten thousand* of them. There were such crowds that the bakeries ran out of bread. And because the inns were full, people spent the night outside: to see this man die, *they slept in the snow.*

And we shake our heads over the Roman gladiators. Oh, charlatans!

A Note from the Paperboy

She tries to get her husband to look at the dog and the cat lying stretched out together companionably side by side on the floor. He is immediately annoyed with her because he is trying to concentrate on what he is doing.

Since he won't talk to her, she then starts talking to the cat and the dog. Again he tells her to be quiet—he can't concentrate.

What he is doing is writing a note to the paperboy. He is writing a note in answer to a note they have received from the paperboy.

The paperboy has written that when walking through their yard in the dark in the early morning, he has "met several animals"—"like skunks." He is announcing that from now on, he would prefer to leave the paper outside the yard, "at the back gate entrance."

Now, in response, her husband is writing to the paperboy saying No, they prefer to have the newspaper delivered *as always* to the back porch, and if he can't do that, they will discontinue the paper.

In fact, according to the grammatical construction used by the paperboy in his note, it is the animals themselves who are not only walking through the yard but also delivering the paper.

In the Train Station

The train station is very crowded. People are walking in every direction at once, though some are standing still. A Tibetan Buddhist monk with shaved head and long wine-colored robe is in the crowd, looking worried. I am standing still, watching him. I have plenty of time before my train leaves, because I have just missed a train. The monk sees me watching him. He comes up to me and tells me he is looking for Track 3. I know where the tracks are. I show him the way.

dream

The Moon

I get up out of bed in the night. My room is large, and dark but for the white dog on the floor. I leave the room. The hall-way is wide and long, and filled with an underwater sort of twilight. I reach the doorway of the bathroom and see that it is flooded with bright light. There is a full moon far above, over-head. Its beam is coming in through the window and falling directly on the toilet seat, as if sent by a helpful God.

Then I am back in bed. I have been lying there awake for a while. The room is lighter than it was. The moon is coming around to this side of the building, I think. But no, it is the beginning of dawn.

dream

My Footsteps

I see myself from the back, walking. There are circles of both light and shadow around each of my footsteps. I know that with each step I can now go farther and faster than ever before, so of course I want to spring forward and run. But I am told that I must pause at each step, letting my foot rest on the ground for a moment, if I want it to develop its full power and reach, before taking the next.

dream

How I Read as Quickly as Possible Through My Back Issues of the *TLS*

I do not want to read about the life of Jerry Lewis.

I do want to read about mammalian carnivores.

I do not want to read about a portrait of a castrato.

I do not want to read this poem:
(". . . and so I stood/at the water's edge among electro-
lytes . . .")

I do want to read about the history of the Inca *khipu*.

I do not want to read about:
the history of the panda in China
a dictionary of women in Shakespeare

Do want to read about:
sow bugs
bumblebees

Do not want to read about Ronald Reagan.

Do not want to read this poem:
("What's the point of sitting on a bus/and fuming?")

Do want to read about the creation of the musical *South Pacific*:
("This study will contribute greatly to the still under-written
history of the Broadway musical")

Not interested in:
The Oxford Companion to Canadian Military History

Not interested in (at least not today):
Hitler
London theater productions

Interested in:
the psychology of lying
Anne Carson on the death of her brother
French writers admired by Proust
the poems of Catullus
translations from the Serbian

Not interested in:
the creation of the Statue of Liberty

Interested in:
beer
East Prussia after World War II
philosemitism

Not interested in:
the Archbishop of Canterbury

Not interested in this poem:
("Light dazzles from the grass/over the carnal dune . . .")

Not interested in:
the Anglo-Portuguese establishment
heraldic leopards

Interested in:
the lectures of Borges
Raymond Queneau's *Exercises in Style*
dust jackets in the history of bibliography:
("For the first time, the dust jacket has been given its due
status . . .")

Not interested in:
the friendship of Elgar and Schenker
the work of Alexander Pope
T. S. Eliot's fountain pen

Not interested in:
the Audit Commission

Interested in:
the social value of altruism
the building of the Pont Neuf
the history of daguerreotypes

Not interested in:
a cultural history of the British Census:
("It is salutary to see, from this learned book, that, *mutatis mutandis*, such controversies have plagued the census since its inception . . .")

Not interested in:
a cultural history of the accordion in America
("Squeeze This")

Interested in:
the Southport Lawnmower Museum

Not interested in:
a history of British television criticism
fashion at the Academy Awards:
("How Oscars dress etiquette has changed since the ceremony's inception in 1928")

Not interested in:
Anacaona: The Amazing Adventures of Cuba's First All-Girl Band

Always (or almost always) interested in:
JC's NB and the doings of the Basement Labyrinth

Not interested in—or, well, yes, maybe interested in:
the history of diplomacy
Laura Bush's autobiography

Notes During Long Phone Conversation with Mother

for summer   she needs
pretty dress   cotton

cotton   nottoc
     coontt
     tcoont
          toonct
     tocnot   tocont
     tocton
   contot

Men

There are also men in the world. Sometimes we forget, and think there are only women—endless hills and plains of unresisting women. We make little jokes and comfort each other and our lives pass quickly. But every now and then, it is true, a man rises unexpectedly in our midst like a pine tree, and looks savagely at us, and sends us hobbling away in great floods to hide in the caves and gullies until he is gone.

Negative Emotions

A well-meaning teacher, inspired by a text he had been reading, once sent all the other teachers in his school a message about negative emotions. The message consisted entirely of advice quoted from a Vietnamese Buddhist monk.

Emotion, said the monk, is like a storm: it stays for a while and then it goes. Upon perceiving the emotion (like a coming storm), one should put oneself in a stable position. One should sit or lie down. One should focus on one's abdomen. One should focus, specifically, on the area just below one's navel, and practice mindful breathing. If one can identify the emotion as an emotion, it may then be easier to handle.

The other teachers were puzzled. They did not understand why their colleague had sent them a message about negative emotions. They resented the message, and they resented their colleague. They thought he was accusing them of having negative emotions and needing advice about how to handle them. Some of them were, in fact, angry.

The teachers did not choose to regard their anger as a coming storm. They did not focus on their abdomens. They did not focus on the area just below their navels. Instead, they wrote back immediately, declaring that because they did not understand why he had sent it, his message had filled them with negative emotions. They told him that it would take a lot of practice for them to get over the negative emotions caused by his message. But, they went on, they did not intend to do this practice. Far from being troubled by their negative emotions, they said, they in fact liked having negative emotions, particularly about him and his message.

I'm Pretty Comfortable,
But I Could Be a Little
More Comfortable

I'm tired.

The people in front of us are taking a long time choosing their ice cream.

My thumb hurts.

A man is coughing during the concert.

The shower is a little too cold.

The work I have to do this morning is difficult.

They have seated us too close to the kitchen.

There's a long line at the shipping counter.

•

I'm cold sitting in the car.

The cuff of my sweater is damp.

The shower is weak.

I'm hungry.

They're quarreling again.

This soup doesn't have much taste.

My navel orange is a little dry.

I didn't get two seats to myself on the train.

He is keeping me waiting.

They have gone off and left me alone at the dinner table.

She says my breathing is incorrect.

I need to go to the bathroom, but someone is in there.

I'm a little tense.

The back of my neck feels prickly.

The cat has ringworm.

The person behind me on the train is eating something very smelly.

It's too hot in that room for me to practice the piano.

He calls me when I'm working.

I bought sour cream by mistake.

My fork is too short.

I'm so tired I won't do well at my lesson.

This apple has brown spots on it.

I ordered a dry corn muffin, but when it came, it wasn't dry.

He chews so loudly I have to turn on the radio.

This pesto is hard to blend.

The wart on my thumb is growing back.

I can't have anything to eat or drink this morning because of the test.

She has parked her Mercedes across the end of my driveway.

I ordered an oat bran raisin muffin lightly toasted, but it wasn't lightly toasted.

My tea water takes too long to boil.

The seam in the toe of my sock is twisted.

It's too cold in that room for me to practice the piano.

He doesn't pronounce foreign words correctly.

My tea is too milky.

I've been in the kitchen too long.

There's cat saliva on my new sock.

My seat doesn't have a back.

The blender is leaking at the bottom.

I can't decide whether to go on reading this book.

I missed the view of the river from the train because it got dark.

The raspberries are sour.

The pepper grinder doesn't grind very well.

The cat has peed on my telephone.

My Band-Aid is wet.

The store is out of decaf hazelnut coffee.

My sheets get all twisted in the dryer.

The carrot cake was a little stale.

When I toast the raisin bread, the raisins get very hot.

The bridge of my nose is a little dry.

I'm sleepy, but I can't lie down.

The sound system in the examining room is playing folk music.

I don't look forward very much to that sandwich.

They have a new weatherman on the radio.

Now that the leaves are off the trees, we can see the neighbor's new deck.

I don't think I like my bedspread anymore.

In the restaurant they are playing a loop of soft rock music.

•

My glasses frames are cold.

There is St. André cheese on the platter, but I can't have any.

The clock is ticking very loudly.

Judgment

Into how small a space the word *judgment* can be compressed:
it must fit inside the brain of a ladybug as she, before my eyes,
makes a decision.

The Chairs

story from Flaubert

Louis has been in the church in Mantes looking at the chairs.
He has been looking at them very closely. He wants to learn as
much as he can about the people from looking at their chairs,
he says. He started with the chair of a woman he calls Madame
Fricotte. Maybe her name was written on the back of the chair.
She must be very stout, he says—the seat of the chair has a deep
hollow in it, and the prayer stool has been reinforced in a couple
of places. Her husband may be a rich man, because the prayer
stool is upholstered in red velvet with brass tacks. Or, he thinks,
the woman may be the widow of a rich man, because there is
no chair belonging to Monsieur Fricotte—unless he's an atheist.
In fact, perhaps Madame Fricotte, if she is a widow, is looking
for another husband, since the back of her chair is heavily stained
with hair dye.

My Friend's Creation

We are in a clearing at night. Along one side, four Egyptian goddesses of immense size are positioned in profile and lit from behind. Black shapes of people come into the clearing and slip across the silhouettes. A moon is pasted against the dark sky. High up on a pole sits a cheerful, red-cheeked man who sings and plays a pipe. Now and then, he climbs down from his pole. He is my friend's creation, and my friend asks me, "What shall he be singing?"

dream

The Piano

We are about to buy a new piano. Our old upright has a crack all the way through the sounding board, and other problems. We would like the piano shop to take it and resell it, but they tell us it is too badly damaged and cannot be resold to anyone else. They say it will have to be pushed over a cliff. This is how they will do it: Two truck drivers take it to a remote spot. One driver walks away down the lane with his back turned while the other shoves it over the cliff.

dream

The Party

A friend and I are on our way to some sort of grand festivity. I am riding in the car of someone I do not know who is vaguely familiar to me. My friend is ahead of us in a different car, a white one. We drive for what seems like hours through deserted streets, making for a hill at the edge of the city. We keep losing our way and stopping to ask directions, because the map that has been given to us is imprecise and hard to read.

At last we come to the top of a steep incline, go on up a curving driveway lit by lanterns among the trees, and come to a stop under a lofty, flood-lit, stone windmill. We leave the cars and walk across the gravel past noisy fountains. The suburbs of the city are spread out below and behind us. We enter the windmill. Inside, a small woman dressed in black and white guides us down whitewashed stairwells, along stone corridors, around several corners, and finally down one last, broader flight of stairs.

At the bottom is a vast, circular room, its raftered ceiling lost in darkness. Filling the room nearly to its edges, and dwarfing the crowd of guests who have arrived before us, is a giant carousel, motionless and crossed by powerful beams of light: white horses, four abreast, are harnessed to open carriages that rock back and forth on their bases; a ship with two figureheads rises high out of static green waves. Around the carousel, the guests shrink back from it, sipping champagne with timid smiles.

We are so surprised that we have not yet moved from the bottom of the steps. Now, though the carousel is still motionless, the calliope begins bleating and gurgling with a deafening noise and the room shudders. A woman with a handbag over her arm approaches one of the horses and stares at its bulging eye. One by one, the guests mount the carousel, not eagerly or happily, but fearfully.

dream

The Cows

Each new day, when they come out from the far side of the barn, it is like the next act, or the start of an entirely new play.

They amble into view from the far side of the barn with their rhythmic, graceful walk, and it is an occasion, like the start of a parade.

Sometimes the second and third come out in stately procession after the first has stopped and stands still, staring.

They come from behind the barn as though something is going to happen, and then nothing happens.

Or we pull back the curtain in the morning and they are already there, in the early sunlight.

They are a deep, inky black. It is a black that swallows light.
    Their bodies are entirely black, but they have white on their faces. On the faces of two of them, there are large patches of

white, like a mask. On the face of the third, there is only a small patch on the forehead, the size of a silver dollar.

They are motionless until they move again, one foot and then another—fore, hind, fore, hind—and stop in another place, motionless again.

So often they are standing completely still. Yet when I look up again a few minutes later, they are in another place, again standing completely still.

When they all three stand bunched together in a far corner of the field by the woods, they form one dark irregular mass, with twelve legs.

They are often crowded together in the large field. But sometimes they lie down far apart from one another, evenly spaced over the grass.

Today, two appear halfway out from behind the barn, standing still. Ten minutes go by. Now they are all the way out, standing still. Another ten minutes go by. Now the third is out and they are all three in a line, standing still.

The third comes out into the field from behind the barn when the other two have already chosen their spots, quite far apart. She can choose to join either one. She goes deliberately to the one in the far corner. Does she prefer the company of that cow, or does she prefer that corner, or is it more complicated—that that corner seems more appealing because of the presence of that cow?

Their attention is complete, as they look across the road: They are still, and face us.

Just because they are so still, their attitude seems philosophical.

I see them most often out the kitchen window over the top of a hedge. My view of them is bounded on either side by leafy trees. I am surprised that the cows are so often visible, because the portion of the hedge over which I see them is only about three feet long, and, even more puzzling, if I hold my arm straight out in front of me, the field of my vision in which they are grazing is only the length of half a finger. Yet that field of vision contains a part of their grazing field that is hundreds of square feet in area.

That one's legs are moving, but because she is facing us directly she seems to be staying in one place. Yet she is getting bigger, so she must be coming this way.

One of them is in the foreground and two are farther back, in the middle ground between her and the woods. In my field of vision, they occupy together in the middle ground the same amount of space she occupies alone in the foreground.

Because there are three, one of them can watch what the other two are doing together.

Or, because there are three, two can worry about the third, for instance the one lying down. They worry about her even though she often lies down, even though they all often lie down. Now the two worried ones stand at angles to the other, with their noses down against her, until at last she gets up.

They are nearly the same size, and yet one is the largest, one the middle-sized, and one the smallest.

One thinks there is a reason to walk briskly to the far corner of the field, but another thinks there is no reason, and stands still where she is.

At first she stands still where she is, while the first walks away briskly, but then she changes her mind and follows.

She follows, but stops halfway there. Is it that she has forgotten why she was going there, or that she has lost interest? She and the other are standing in parallel positions. She is looking straight ahead.

How often they stand still and slowly look around as though they have never been here before.

But now, in an access of emotion, she trots a few feet.

I see only one cow, by the fence. As I walk up to the fence, I see part of a second cow: one ear sticking sideways out the door of the barn. Soon, I know, her whole face will appear, looking at me.

They are not disappointed in us, or do not remember being disappointed. If, one day, when we have nothing to offer them, they lose interest and turn away, they will have forgotten their disappointment by the next day. We know, because they look up when we first appear and don't look away.

Sometimes they advance as a group, in little relays.

One gains courage from the one in front of her and moves forward a few steps, passing her by just a little. Now the one farthest back gains courage from the one in front and moves forward until she, in turn, is the leader. And so in this way, taking courage from one another, they advance, as a group, towards the strange thing in front of them.

In this, functioning as a single entity, they are not unlike the small flock of pigeons we sometimes see over the railway station, wheeling and turning in the sky continuously, making immediate small group decisions about where to go next.

When we come close to them, they are curious and come forward. They want to look at us and smell us. Before they smell us, they blow out forcefully, to clear their passages.

They like to lick things—a person's hand or sleeve, or the head or shoulders or back of another cow. And they like to be licked: while she is being licked, she stands very still with her head slightly lowered and a look of deep concentration in her eyes.

One may be jealous of another being licked: she thrusts her head under the outstretched neck of the one licking, and butts upwards till the licking stops.

Two of them are standing close together: now they both move at the same moment, shifting into a different position in relation to each other, and then stand still again, as if following exactly the instructions of a choreographer.

Now they shift so that there is a head at either end and two thick clusters of legs in between.

After staying with the others in a tight clump for some time, one walks away by herself to the far corner of the field: at this moment, she does seem to have a mind of her own.

Lying down, seen from the side, her head up, feet bent in front of her, she forms a long, acute triangle.

Her head, from the side, is nearly an isosceles triangle, with a blunted corner where her nose is.

In a moment of solitary levity, as she leads the way out across the field, she bucks once and then prances.

Two of them are beginning a lively game of butt-your-head when a car goes by and they stop to look.

She bucks, stiffly rocking back and forth. This excites another one to butt heads with her. After they are done butting heads, the other one puts her nose back down to the ground and this one stands still, looking straight ahead, as though wondering what she just did.

Forms of play: head-butting; mounting, either at the back or at the front; trotting away by yourself; trotting together; going off bucking and prancing by yourself; resting your head and chest on the ground until they notice and trot towards you; circling one another; taking the position for head-butting and then not doing it.

She moos towards the wooded hills behind her, and the sound comes back. She moos again in a high falsetto. It is a very small sound to come from such a large, dark animal.

Today, they are positioned exactly one behind the next in a line, head to tail, head to tail, as though coupled like the cars of a railway train, the first looking straight forward like the headlight of the locomotive.

The shape of a black cow, seen directly head-on: a smooth black oval, larger at the top and tapering at the bottom to a very narrow extension, like a teardrop.

Standing with their back ends close together now, they face three of the four cardinal points of the compass.

Sometimes one takes the position for defecating, her tail, raised at the base, in the curved shape of a pump handle.

They seem expectant this morning, but it is a combination of two things: the strange yellow light before a storm and their alert expressions as they listen to a loud woodpecker.

Spaced out evenly over the pale yellow-green grass of late November, one, two, and three, they are so still, and their legs so thin, in comparison to their bodies, that when they stand sideways to us, sometimes their legs seem like prongs, and they seem stuck to the earth.

How flexible, and how precise, she is: she can reach one of her back hooves all the way forward, to scratch a particular spot inside her ear.

It is the lowered head that makes her seem less noble than, say, a horse, or a deer surprised in the woods. More exactly, it is her lowered head and neck. As she stands still, the top of her head is level with her back, or even a little lower, and so she seems to be hanging her head in discouragement, embarrassment, or shame. There is at least a suggestion of humility and dullness about her. But all these suggestions are false.

He says to us: They don't really do anything.
    Then he adds: But of course there is not a lot for them to do.

Their grace: as they walk, they are more graceful when seen from the side than when seen from the front. Seen from the front, as they walk, they tip just a little from side to side.

When they are walking, their forelegs are more graceful than their back legs, which appear stiffer.

The forelegs are more graceful than the back legs because they lift in a curve, whereas the back legs lift in a jagged line like a bolt of lightning.

But perhaps the back legs, while less graceful than the forelegs, are more elegant.

It is because of the way the joints in the legs work: Whereas the two lower joints of the front leg bend the same way, so that the front leg as it is raised forms a curve, the two lower joints of the back leg bend in opposite directions, so that the leg, when raised, forms two opposite angles, the lower one gentle, pointing forward, the upper one sharp, pointing back.

Now, because it is winter, they are not grazing but only standing still and staring, or, now and then, walking here and there.

It is a very cold winter morning, just above zero degrees, but sunny. Two of them stand still, head to tail, for a very long time, oriented roughly east-west. They are probably presenting their broad sides to the sun, for warmth.

If they finally move, is it because they are warm enough, or is it that they are stiff, or bored?

They are sometimes a mass of black, a lumpy black clump, against the snow, with a head at either end and many legs below.

Or the three of them, seen from the side, when they are all facing the same way, three deep, make one thick cow with three heads, two up and one lowered.

Sometimes, what we see against the snow is their bumps—bumps of ears and nose, bumps of bony hips, or the sharp bone on the top of their heads, or their shoulders.

If it snows, it snows on them the same way it snows on the trees and the field. Sometimes they are just as still as the trees or the field. The snow piles up on their backs and heads.

It has been snowing heavily for some time, and it is still snowing. When we go up to them, where they stand by the fence, we see that there is a layer of snow on their backs. There is also a layer of snow on their faces, and even a thin line of snow on each of the whiskers around their mouths. The snow on their faces is so white that now the white patches on their faces, which once looked so white against their black, are a shade of yellow.

Against the snow, in the distance, coming head-on this way, separately, spaced far apart, they are like wide black strokes of a pen.

A winter's day: First, a boy plays in the snow in the same field as the cows. Then, outside the field, three boys throw snowballs at a fourth boy who rides past them on a bike.

Meanwhile, the three cows are standing end to end, each touching the next, like paper cutouts.

Now the boys begin to throw snowballs at the cows. A neighbor watching says: "It was only a matter of time. They were bound to do it."

But the cows merely walk away from the boys.

They are so black on the white snow and standing so close together that I don't know if there are three there, together, or just two—but surely there are more than eight legs in that bunch?

At a distance, one bows down into the snow; the other two watch, then begin to trot towards her, then break into a canter.

At the far edge of the field, next to the woods, they are walking from right to left, and because of where they are, their dark bodies entirely disappear against the dark woods behind them, while their legs are still visible against the snow—black sticks twinkling against the white ground.

They are often like a math problem: 2 cows lying down in the snow, plus 1 cow standing up looking at the hill, equals 3 cows.

Or: 1 cow lying down in the snow, plus 2 cows on their feet looking this way across the road, equals 3 cows.

Today, they are all three lying down.

Now, in the heart of winter, they spend a lot of time lying around in the snow.

•

Does she lie down because the other two have lain down before her, or are they all three lying down because they all feel it is the right time to lie down? (It is just after noon, on a chilly, early spring day, with intermittent sun and no snow on the ground.)

Is the shape of her lying down, when seen from the side, most of all like a bootjack as seen from above?

It is hard to believe a life could be so simple, but it is just this simple. It is the life of a ruminant, a protected domestic ruminant. If she were to give birth to a calf, though, her life would be more complicated.

The cows in the past, the present, and the future: They were so black against the pale yellow-green grass of late November. Then they were so black against the white snow of winter. Now they are so black against the tawny grass of early spring. Soon, they will be so black against the dark green grass of summer.

Two of them are probably pregnant, and have probably been pregnant for many months. But it is hard to be sure, because they are so massive. We won't know until the calf is born. And after the calf is born, even though it will be quite large, the cow will seem to be just as massive as she was before.

The angles of a cow as she grazes, seen from the side: from her bony hips to her shoulders, there is a very gradual, barely perceptible slope down; then, from her shoulders to the tip of her nose, down in the grass, a very steep slope.

•

The position, or form, itself, of the grazing cow, when seen from the side, is graceful.

Why do they so often graze side-view on to me, rather than front- or rear-view on? Is it so that they can keep an eye on both the woods, on one side, and the road, on the other? Or does the traffic on the road, sparse though it is, right to left and left to right, influence them so that they graze parallel to it?

Or perhaps it isn't true that they graze more often sideways on to me. Maybe I simply pay more attention to them when they are sideways on. After all, when they are perfectly sideways on, to me, the greatest surface area of their bodies is visible to me; as soon as the angle changes, I see less of them, until, when they are perfectly end-on or front-on to me, the least of them is visible.

They make slow progress here and there in the field, with only their tails moving briskly from side to side. In contrast, little flocks of birds—as black as they are—fly up and land constantly in waves behind and around them. The birds move with what looks to us like joy or exhilaration but is probably simply keenness in pursuit of their prey—the flies that in turn dart out from the cows and settle on them again.

Their tails do not exactly whip or flap, and they do not swish, since there is no swishing sound. There is a swooping or looping motion to them, with a little fillip at the end, from the tasseled part.

•

Her head is down, and she is grazing in a circle of darkness that is her own shadow.

Just as it is hard for us, in our garden, to stop weeding, because there is always another weed there in front of us, it may be hard for her to stop grazing, because there are always a few more shoots of fresh grass just ahead of her.

If the grass is short, she may grasp it directly between her teeth and her lip; if the grass is longer, she may capture it first with a sideways sweep of her tongue, in order to bring it into her mouth.

Their large tongues are not pink. The tongues of two of them are light gray. The tongue of the third, the darkest one, is dark gray.

One of them has given birth to a calf. But in fact her life is not much more complicated than it was before. She stands still to let him nurse. She licks him.

Only the hours of the birth itself, on that day (Palm Sunday), were much more complicated.

Today, again, the cows are positioned symmetrically in the field, but now there is a short stray line of dark in the grass among them—the calf sleeping.

There used to be three dark horizontal lumps on the field when they lay down to rest. Now there are three and another very small one.

Soon he, three days old, is grazing, too, or learning to graze, but so small, from where I stand watching him, that he is sometimes hidden by a twig.

When he stands still, a miniature, nose to the grass like his mother, because his body is so small and his legs so thin, he looks like a thick black staple.

When he runs after her, he canters like a rocking horse.

They do sometimes protest—when they have no water or can't get into the barn. One of them, the darkest, will moo in a perfectly regular blast twenty or more times in succession. The sound echoes off the hills like a fire alarm coming from a firehouse.

At these times, she sounds authoritative. But she has no authority.

A second calf is born, to a second cow. Now one small dark lump in the grass is the older calf. Another, smaller dark lump in the grass is the newborn calf.

The third cow could not be bred because she would not get into the van to be taken to the bull. Then, after a few months, they wanted to take her to be slaughtered. But she would not get into the van to be taken to slaughter. So she is still there.

Other neighbors may be away, from time to time, but the cows are always there, in the field. Or, if they are not in the field, they are in the barn.

I know that if they are in the field, and if I go up to the fence on this side, they will, all three, sooner or later come up to the fence on the other side, to meet me.

They do not know the words *person*, *neighbor*, *watch*, or even *cow*.

At dusk, when our light is on indoors, they can't be seen, though they are there in the field across the road. If we turn off the light and look out into the dusk, gradually they can be seen again.

They are still out there, grazing, at dusk. But as the dusk turns to dark, while the sky above the woods is still a purplish blue, it is harder and harder to see their black bodies against the darkening field. Then they can't be seen at all, but they are still out there, grazing in the dark.

The Exhibition

story from Flaubert

Yesterday, in the deep snow, I went to an exhibition of savages that had come here from Le Havre. They were Kaffirs. The poor Negroes, and their manager too, looked as if they were dying of hunger.

You paid a few pennies to get into the exhibition. It was in a miserable smoke-filled room up several flights of stairs. It was not well attended—seven or eight fellows in work clothes sat here and there in the rows of chairs. We waited for some time. Then a sort of wild beast appeared wearing a tiger skin on his back and uttering harsh cries. A few more followed him into the room—there were four altogether. They got up on a platform and crouched around a stew pot. Hideous and splendid at the same time, they were covered with amulets and tattoos, as thin as skeletons, their skin the color of my well-seasoned old pipe; their faces were flat, their teeth white, their eyes large, their expressions desperately sad, astonished, and brutalized. The twilight outside the windows, and the snow whitening the rooftops across the street, cast a gray pall over them. I felt as though I were seeing the first men on earth—as though they had just come into existence and were creeping about with the toads and the crocodiles.

Then one of them, an old woman, noticed me and came into the audience where I was sitting—she had, it seems, taken a sudden liking to me. She said some things to me—affectionate things, as far as I could tell. Then she tried to kiss me. The audience watched in surprise. For a quarter of an hour I stayed there in my seat listening to her long declaration of love. I asked the manager several times what she was saying, but he couldn't translate any of it.

Though he claimed they knew a little English, they didn't seem to understand a word, because after the show at last came to an end—to my relief—I asked them a few questions and they couldn't answer. I was glad to leave that dismal place and go back out into the snow, though I had lost my boots somewhere.

What is it that makes me so attractive to cretins, madmen, idiots, and savages? Do those poor creatures sense a kind of sympathy in me? Do they feel some sort of bond between us? It is *infallible*. It happened with the cretins of Valais, the madmen of Cairo, the monks of Upper Egypt—they all persecuted me with their declarations of love!

Later, I heard that after this exhibition of savages, their manager abandoned them. They had been in Rouen for nearly two months by then, first on the boulevard Beauvoisin, then in the Grande-Rue, where I saw them. When he left, they were living in a shabby little hotel in the rue de la Vicomté. Their only recourse was to take their case to the English consul—I don't know how they made themselves understood. But the consul paid their debts—400 francs to the hotel—and then put them on the train for Paris. They had an engagement there—it was to be their Paris debut.

Letter to a Peppermint Candy Company

Dear Manufacturer of "Old Fashioned Chewy Peps,"

Last Christmas when my husband and I stopped in at an upscale country store that caters to weekenders as well as locals and has a lunchroom off to the side, and which is run by a couple who bicker constantly and snap at their help, after we had had lunch and were browsing, before we left, among the displays of packaged and freshly prepared gourmet foods, we were attracted to the festive bright red canister (what you call the "tin") of your "Old Fashioned Chewy Peps" peppermints. I love peppermints, and when I read the ingredients list on your can and saw that these were made without preservatives or artificial flavors or colors, I decided to buy the peppermints, since it is hard to find pure candies. I did not ask the price of the can, because although I realized that in that particular store it would be expensive, I was willing to be a bit extravagant since Christmas was coming. When I went to pay, though, I was shocked at the price, which was $15 for the canister of peppermints, net weight 13 ounces (369 grams). After a moment of hesitation, I bought it anyway, partly out of embarrassment in front of the impatient and unsmiling young woman at the cash register and partly because I did not want to give up those peppermints. When we got home, I read your tongue-in-cheek warning on the can about letting the peppermint soften in one's mouth before biting down. You said: "Your teeth will thank you!" Well, it is quite true that the peppermints appear soft but then have an iron grip when one bites down. When I did eventually eat one, I chewed cautiously and with great difficulty. The candy was quite awkward to hold in my mouth, since it kept sticking to one tooth or another. I will say right away, though, that the taste was excellent. What I am writing to you about is not the taste or the difficulty of chewing the mints but the quantity of mints in the canister. When I first opened it, before I ate any of the peppermints, I noticed that it did not seem to be very tightly packed with candies. They filled it to the top, but loosely. I looked at the ingredients list again. I saw that you reported a serving size of 6 pieces and then specified that there were "about" 12⅓ servings per tin. I did the math and calculated that the tin should contain "about" 74 pieces. Frankly, I did not think there were 74 pieces of candy inside. After I pointed this out to my family, we decided to place bets on how many candies there were and then count them. My bet was 64 pieces. My husband, being more trusting of your claims, bet that there were 70. My son, being a teenager and more daring, bet that there were only 50 pieces. Well, I counted them out there on the dining table and who do you think won the bet? I'm sorry to say it was my son. There were only 51 pieces in the can (or tin)! I must say, I could understand it if there were 70 or even 66 pieces, but 51 pieces is only two-thirds, approximately, of the number of pieces you claim are in the tin. I don't really understand why you would make such a false claim. I have just now, out of curiosity, done a calculation to see if your claim as to the net weight of the peppermints is also exaggerated. You claim that each piece weighs about 5 grams, and you claim a net weight of 369 grams. Yet that would also yield 74 pieces, rounding up, and since there were not 74 pieces but 51, the net weight of the peppermints would have been closer to 255 grams. I cannot verify this estimate by weighing the candies because by now we have eaten them all. They were delicious, but we are feeling short-changed, or should I say . . . cheated? Can you please explain this discrepancy?

Yours sincerely.

P.S. This also makes my purchase even more extravagant. 13 ounces at $15 would have been about $18/pound; 8 ounces at $15 is $30/pound!

Her Geography: Illinois

She knows she is in Chicago.
But she does not yet realize that she is in Illinois.

IV

Ödön von Horváth Out Walking

Ödön von Horváth was once walking in the Bavarian Alps when he discovered, at some distance from the path, the skeleton of a man. The man had evidently been a hiker, since he was still wearing a knapsack. Von Horváth opened the knapsack, which looked almost as good as new. In it, he found a sweater and other clothing; a small bag of what had once been food; a diary; and a picture postcard of the Bavarian Alps, ready to send, that read, "Having a wonderful time."

On the Train

We are united, he and I, though strangers, against the two women in front of us talking so steadily and audibly across the aisle to each other. Bad manners. We frown.

Later in the journey I look over at him (across the aisle) and he is picking his nose. As for me, I am dripping tomato from my sandwich onto my newspaper. Bad habits.

I would not report this if I were the one picking my nose.
I look again and he is still at it.

As for the women, they are now sitting together side by side and quietly reading, clean and tidy, one a magazine, one a book. Blameless.

The Problem of the Vacuum Cleaner

A priest is about to come visit us—or maybe it is two priests.

But the maid has left the vacuum cleaner in the hall, directly in front of the front door.

I have asked her twice to take it away, but she will not.

I certainly will not.

One of the priests, I know, is the Rector of Patagonia.

The Seals

I know we're supposed to be happy on this day. How odd that is. When you're very young, you're usually happy, at least you're ready to be. You get older and see things more clearly and there's less to be happy about. Also, you start losing people— your family. Ours weren't necessarily easy, but they were ours, the hand we were dealt. There were five of us, actually, like a poker hand—I never thought of that before.

We're beyond the river and into New Jersey now, we'll be in Philadelphia in about an hour, we pulled out of the station on time.

I'm thinking especially about her—older than me and older than our brother, and so often responsible for us, always the most responsible, at least till we were all grown up. By the time I was grown up, she already had her first child. Actually, by the time I was twenty-one, she had both of them.

Most of the time I don't think about her, because I don't like to feel sad. Her broad cheeks, soft skin, lovely features, large eyes, her light complexion, blond hair, colored but natural, with a little gray in it. She always looked a little tired, a little sad, when she paused in a conversation, when she rested for a moment, and especially in a photograph. I've searched and searched for a photo in which she doesn't look tired or sad, but I can find only one.

They said she looked young, and peaceful, in her coma, day after day. It went on and on—no one knew exactly when it would end. My brother told me she had a glow over her face, a damp sheen—she was sweating lightly. The plan was to let her breathe on her own, with a little oxygen, until she stopped breathing. I never saw her in the coma, I never saw her at the end. I'm sorry about that now. I thought I should stay with our mother and wait it out here, holding her hand, till the phone call came. At least that's what I told myself. The phone call came in the middle of the night. My mother and I both got out of bed, and then stood there together in the dark living room, the only light coming from outside, from the streetlamps.

I miss her so much. Maybe you miss someone even more when you can't figure out what your relationship was. Or when it seemed unfinished. When I was little, I thought I loved her more than our mother. Then she left home.

I think she left right after she was done with college. She moved away to the city. I would have been about seven. I have some memories of her in that house, before she moved away. I remember her playing music in the living room, I remember her standing by the piano, bent a little forward, her lips pursed around the mouthpiece of her clarinet, her eyes on the sheet music. She played very well then. There were always little family dramas about the reeds she needed for the mouthpiece of her clarinet. Years later, miles away from there, when I was visiting her, she would bring out the clarinet again, not having played it in a long time, and we would try to play something together, we would work our way, hit or miss, through something. You could sometimes hear the full, round tones that she had learned how to make, and her perfect sense of the shape of a line of music, but the muscles of her lips had weakened and sometimes she lost control. The instrument would squeak or remain silent. Playing, she would force the air into the mouthpiece, pressing hard, and then, when there was a rest, she would lower the instrument for a moment, expel the air in a rush, and then take a quick breath before starting to play again.

I remember where the piano was in our house, just inside

the archway into that long, low-ceilinged room shadowed by pine trees outside the front windows, with sun coming in the side windows, on the open side, from the sunny yard, where the rosebushes grew against the house and the beds of iris lay out in the middle of the lawn, but I don't remember her there on this holiday. Maybe she didn't come home for that. She was too far away to come back very often. We didn't have a lot of money, so there probably wasn't much for train fares. And maybe she didn't want to come back very often. I wouldn't have understood that then. I told our mother I would give up all the few dollars I had saved if it would bring her home again for a visit. I was very serious about this, I thought it would help, but our mother just smiled.

I missed her so much. When she still lived at home she often looked after us, my brother and me. On the day I was born, on that hot summer afternoon, she was the one who stayed with my brother. They were dropped off at the county fair. She led him around the rides and booths for hours and hours, both of them hot and thirsty and tired, in that flat basin of fairground where years later we watched the fireworks. My father and mother were miles away, across town, at the hospital on the top of the hill.

When I was ten, the rest of us moved, too, to the same city, so for a few years we all lived close by. She would come over to our apartment and stay for a while, but I don't think she came very often, and I don't really understand why not. I don't remember family meals together with her, I don't remember excursions in the city together. At the apartment, she would listen carefully when I practiced the piano. She would tell me when I played a wrong note, but sometimes she was wrong about that. She taught me my first word in French: she made me say it over and over till I had the pronunciation just right. Our mother is gone now, too, so I can't ask her why we didn't see her more often.

There won't be any more animal-themed presents from her. There won't be any more presents from her at all.

Why those animal-themed presents? Why did she want to remind me of animals? She once gave me a mobile made of china penguins—why? Another time, a seagull of balsa wood that hung on strings and bobbed its wings up and down in the breeze. Another time, a dish towel with badgers on it. I still have that. Why badgers?

Trenton Makes, the World Takes—out the window. How many advertising slogans will I stare at out the window today? Now there are poles falling over into the water with all their wires still strung on them—what happened to them, and why were they left there?

It's always the ones without families who get asked to work on this day. I could have claimed that I was spending it with my brother, but he's in Mexico.

Four hours, a little more. I'll be there around dinnertime. I'll eat in the hotel restaurant, if there is one. That's always the easiest. The food is never really very good, but the people are friendly. They have to be, it's part of their job. Friendly sometimes meaning they'll turn the music down for me. Or they'll say they can't, but smile.

Was a love of animals something we shared? She must have liked them or she wouldn't have sent me those presents. I can't remember how she was with animals. I try to remember her different moods: so often worried, sometimes more relaxed and smiling (at the table, after a drink of wine), sometimes laughing at a joke, sometimes playful (years ago, with her children), at those times filled with sudden physical energy, lunging at someone across the lawn, under the bay tree, in the walled garden that her husband cared for so patiently.

She worried about so many things. She would imagine a bad outcome and she would elaborate on it until it grew into a story and moved far away from where it started. It could start with a prediction of rain. To one of her grown daughters, she might say something like It's going to rain. Don't forget your raincoat. If you get wet you might catch cold, and then you might miss the performance tomorrow. That would be too bad. Bill would be so disappointed. He's looking forward to hearing what you think of the play. You and he have talked about it so much . . .

I think about that a lot—how tense she was. It's something that must have started very early, she had such a complicated childhood. Three fathers by the time she was six years old—or two, I suppose, if you don't count her actual father. He knew her only when she was a baby. Our mother kept leaving her with other people—a nanny, a cousin. For a morning or a day, usually, but once, at least, for weeks and weeks. Our mother had to work—it was always for a good reason.

I didn't see her often, a long time would go by, because she lived so far away. When we saw each other again, she would put her arms around me and give me a strong hug, pressing me against her soft chest, my cheek against her shoulder. She was half a head taller, and she was broader. I was not only younger, but smaller. She had been there as long as I could remember. I always felt she would protect me or look out for me, even when I was grown up. I still sometimes think, with a pang of longing, before I realize what I'm thinking, that some older woman I see somewhere, about fourteen years older, will take care of me. When she drew back from hugging me, she would be looking off to the side or over my head. She seemed to be thinking of something else. Then, when her eyes rested on me, I wasn't sure she saw me. I didn't know what her feelings for me really were.

What was my place in her life? I sometimes thought that to her daughters, and even to her, I didn't matter. The sensation would come over me suddenly, an emptiness, as if I didn't even exist. There were just the three of them, her two girls and her, after their father died, after her second husband left. I was peripheral, our brother was, too, though he and I had been such a large part of her life early on.

I was never sure how she felt about anyone except her daughters. I could tell how much she missed them, when they were away, because she would suddenly become so quiet. Or when they were about to go away—from the rented house at the beach, saying goodbye on the front doorstep, the shiny dune grass growing in the sand beyond the cars, the gray shingle of the roof in the sun, the smell of fish and creosote, the sun reflecting off the cars, then the slam of one car door, the slam of the other car door, and her silence as she watched. It was when she was quiet that I felt I had more access to the truth of her feelings, a way to see into them, and those times were mostly in relation to her daughters.

But I think her feelings about our mother were a heavy burden in her life, at least when they were together. When our mother was far away, maybe she could forget her. Our mother was always stepping on her to get up higher, always needing to be right, always needing to be better than her, and than all of us, most of the time. The terrible innocence of our mother, too, as she did that. She had no idea, most of the time.

Our last conversation—it was on the phone, long-distance. She said she was having trouble seeing things on the right side of her field of vision. On a form she was filling out, she saw the word *date* and wrote in the day's date, not seeing that there were more words to the right of it, and that she was supposed to fill in *date of birth*. We talked for a while, and towards the end of the conversation, I must have said something about talking again in a few days, or staying in touch about her condition, because then, in answer to that, she said she didn't want to talk again, because she wanted to save all her strength for talking to her daughters. As she said it, her voice sounded to me distant, or exhausted, she did not soften what she was saying, or apologize. We never talked again after that. I felt pushed away, pushed out of her life. But her coolness was the sound of her own fear, her preoccupation with what was happening to her, not anything against me.

After she died, I kept going over and over it, trying to see what she felt about me, trying to measure it, find the affection or the love, measure that, make sure of it. She must have had mixed feelings about me, her much younger sister—my life at home was easier than hers had ever been. She probably felt some jealousy that went on and on, year after year, and yet she did want to be with me, she came to where I lived, she visited me, she slept in my living room, it was two nights, at least. She came more than once. Was it on one of those visits that I heard her little radio going half the night, close beside her next to the bed, muttering and singing, or was it in one of the rented beach places during the summer vacation, sand on the floor, someone else's furniture, someone else's art on the walls? She had trouble sleeping, she kept the radio on and read a detective novel late into the night.

And she did have me come and stay with her, and once I lived with her for a while, when I had to get away from my parents. Sometimes I thought she took me in from a sense of duty to me, her younger sister, since I was always having my own problems.

She always sent our package well ahead of time. Inside, each present was wrapped in soft tissue paper, or stiffer wrapping paper. All these presents—she picked them out, bought them, wrapped them in cheerful paper, labeled them in her large script with black or colored marker directly on the gift wrap, and sent them a couple of weeks in advance.

I know I always cared too much about my presents. This holiday was the high point of the year for me when I was a child, and that has never changed. The year culminates in this holiday and the turning of the old year to the new year, and then the circle of the year begins again, always leading up to this holiday.

The seagull ended up in a closet, the strings tangled. From time to time, I would try to untangle it, and at last I succeeded. Then I hung it from a rafter in the barn with a piece of duct tape. After a while, in the heat of the summer, the tape loosened and it fell down.

Then there was that little green stuffed elephant with sequins, from India, quite pretty. With two little cords on it, to hang it up somewhere. I hung it in a window and the green material on one side of it faded after a while in the sunlight. And a thing made of felt, with pockets, to hang on the back of a door and put things in—I'm not sure what. It had elephants on it, too, embroidered on the felt.

Now I remember—she would get these things at special handicraft fairs to benefit some organization of indigenous people. That was part of her kindness, and her conscientiousness, and part of the reason the things were a little odd and sometimes a strange match for us.

So there was always the excitement of her package arriving in the mail. The coarse brown paper a little battered from the trip overseas. The brown paper was even more exciting than the wrappings inside, because it was so drab, yet you knew that inside there would be that explosion of little packages, each wrapped in bright colored paper.

She chose my presents with me in mind, I think, but twisting the facts a little, in an optimistic sort of way, thinking I would find this thing useful or decorative. I think a lot of people, when they pick out a gift, twist the facts optimistically. But I'm not saying I'm against people trying out a different kind of gift on someone, and I'm certainly not against those handicraft fairs. Now that a few years have gone by, and I've changed, too, I would buy my gifts at a handicraft fair. I would do it at least in her memory.

She wouldn't spend a lot of money on a gift. That was her conscience. She wouldn't spend a lot on herself, either. I also believe that deep down, she probably didn't think she deserved any better.

But she spent a lot on us at other times. Her gifts then would come out of the blue. Once, she wrote to me and asked if I wanted to go on a skiing trip in the mountains with her and the children. It was early spring and the snow was melting in muddy patches on the slopes. We skied on what snow there was. I sometimes went off on long walks. She thought I shouldn't go by myself—if something happened to me, I would be alone and without help. But she could not forbid me to go, so I went. On the paths I took, in fact, there were many people hiking up and down, passing one another with a friendly greeting.

Years later, when I was long past the age when I should have needed any help from her, she bought me my first computer. I could have refused, but I still did not have much money. And there was something exciting about her sudden offer one afternoon, over the phone. It was late in the evening where she was. Her offer was an enveloping burst of generosity, I wanted to sink into it and stay inside it. Yes, she said, yes, she insisted, she would send me the money. The next day she called again, a little calmer—she wanted to help, she would send me some money, but not the whole amount, which was a lot in those days. I know how it must have been—late in the evening, she was thinking of me, and missing me, and the feeling grew in her and turned into a desire to do something for me, even something dramatic.

Starting at about that time, she would rent a house for us each summer, or at least pay for most of it, a house at the beach, for a week or two, a different one each year, and we would all go there and be there together. The last time we did this was the last year of my father's life, though he didn't come to the beach house—we left him behind in the nursing home. The next summer, he was gone, and she was gone, too.

Nearly to Philadelphia—rounding the bend, by the river, there are the boathouses on the other side, that big museum on the cliff across the water, like a building from ancient Greece. I won't see the station this time—its high ceiling and long wooden benches and archways and preserved old signs. I could just stand there looking at it for a while, the deep space of it—I do, now and then, if I have time. Our own Penn Station was even grander. It's gone now—that always hurts to think about. And then when you're walking around there in that underground concourse, killing time before your train, you keep passing the photos they put up on the columns, of the old Penn Station, the long shafts of sunlight falling through the tall windows down the flights of marble stairs. As if they want to remind us of what we're missing—strange.

Then we'll be passing through Amish country. I never remember to watch for it, it always takes me by surprise. In the spring, the teams of mules and horses plowing the sloping fields up to the horizon—none of that today. The wash on the lines—maybe. It's cloudy, but dry and windy. What was that I read about salting your wash in winter? Anyway, it's not freezing today. A warm winter.

Again and again, she tried to pay our brother's way over, to go visit her. He never went. He never said why. He finally went when she was dying, when she didn't know it, it was too late for her to have that satisfaction—that at last he had agreed to come. He stayed there until the end. When he was not with her, he walked around the city. He took care of some of the practical things that had to be done. Then he stayed on for the funeral. I did not go over for the funeral. I had good reasons, to me they seemed good, anyway, having to do with our old mother, and the shock of it, and how far away it was, across the ocean. Really, it had more to do with the strangers who would be at the funeral, and the tenderness of my own feelings, which I did not want to share with strangers.

I could share her when she was alive. When she was alive, her presence was endless, time with her was endless, time was endless. Our mother was very old already, and when we children stopped to think about how long we might live, we thought we would live to be just as old. Then, suddenly, there was that strange problem with her vision, which turned out to be a problem not with her vision but in her brain, and then, without warning, the bleeding and the coma, and the doctors announcing that she did not have long to live.

Once she was gone, every memory was suddenly precious, even the bad ones, even the times I was irritated with her, or she was irritated with me. Then it seemed a luxury to be irritated.

I did not want to share her, I did not want to hear a stranger say something about her, a minister in front of the congregation, or a friend of hers who would see her in a different way. To stay with her, in my mind, to remain with her, was not easy, since it was all in my mind, since she wasn't really there, and for that, it had to be just the two of us, no one else. There would have been strangers at the funeral, people she knew but I didn't know, or people I knew but didn't like, people who had cared about her or had not cared about her but thought they should attend the funeral. But now I'm sorry, or rather, I'm sorry I couldn't have done both—gone to the funeral and also stayed home to be with our mother and nurse my own grief and my own memories.

Suddenly, after she was gone, things of hers became more valuable than they had been before—her letters, of course, though there weren't many of them, but also things she had left behind in my house after her last visit, like her jacket, a dark blue windbreaker with some logo on it. A detective novel I tried to read and couldn't. A tub of frozen clams in the freezer, and a jar of tartar sauce, marked down, in the door of the fridge.

We're moving pretty fast now. When you slide by it all so quickly, you think you won't ever have to get bogged down in it again—the traffic, the neighborhoods, the stores, waiting in lines. We're really speeding. The ride is smooth. Just a little squeaking from some metal part in the car that's jiggling. We're all jiggling a little.

There aren't many people in the car, and they're pretty quiet today. I don't mind telling someone if he talks too long on his cell phone. I did that once. I gave this man ten minutes, maybe even more, maybe twenty, and then I went and stood there next to him in the aisle. He was hunched over with his finger pressed against his free ear. He didn't get angry. He looked up at me, smiled, waved his hand in the air, and ended the call before I was back in my seat. I don't do business on my cell phone on the train. They should know better.

There were also gifts of a different kind that she gave—the effort she went to for other people, the work she put into preparing meals for friends. The wanderers she took into her house, to live for weeks or months—kids passing through, but also, one year, that thin old Indian who spent every day arranging her books in the bookcases, and who ate so little and meditated so long. And later her old father, her actual father, the one she first met when she was already grown up, not my father, not the father who raised her. She had had a dream about him, that he was very ill. She had set out to find him, and she had found him.

She was so tired by the end of the day that whenever I

was there visiting, when we all sat watching some program or movie on television in the evening, she would fall asleep. First she was awake for a while, curious about the actors—who is that, didn't we see him in . . . ?—and then she would grow quiet, she was quiet for so long that you would look over and see that her head was leaning to the side, the lamplight shining on her light hair, or her head was bowed over her chest, and she would sleep until we all stood up to go to bed.

What was the last present she gave me? Seven years ago. If I had known it was the last, I would have given it such careful attention.

If it wasn't animal-themed or made by some indigenous person, then it was probably some kind of a bag, not an expensive bag, but one that had a special feature, a trick to it, like it folded into itself when it was empty, and then zipped up and had a little clip on it so you could clip it onto another bag. I have a few of those stored away.

She carried them herself, and other kinds of bags, always open and full of things—an extra sweater, another bag, a couple of books, a box of crackers, a bottle of something to drink. There was a generosity in how much she packed and carried with her.

One time when she came to visit—I'm thinking of her bags leaning in a group against a chair of mine. I was nearly paralyzed, not knowing what to do. I don't know why. I didn't want to leave her alone, that wouldn't have been right, but I also wasn't used to having company. After a while, the panicky feeling passed, maybe just because time passed, but there was a moment when I thought I was going to collapse.

Now I can look at that same bed where she slept and wish she would come back at least for a little while. We wouldn't have to talk, we wouldn't even have to look at each other, but it would be a comfort just to have her there—her arms, her broad shoulders, her hair.

I want to say to her, Yes, there were problems, our relationship was difficult to understand, and complicated, but still, I would like just to have you sitting there on the daybed where you did sleep for a few nights once, it's your part of the living room now, I'd like to just look at your cheeks, your shoulders, your arms, your wrist with the gold watchband on it, a little tight, pressing into the flesh, your strong hands, the gold wedding ring, your short fingernails, I don't have to look you in the eyes or have any sort of communion, complete or incomplete, but to have you there in person, in the flesh, for a while, pressing down the mattress, making folds in the cover, the sun coming in behind you, would be very nice. Maybe you would stretch out on the daybed and read for a while in the afternoon, maybe fall asleep. I would be in the next room, nearby.

Sometimes, after dinner, if she was very relaxed and I was sitting next to her, she would put her hand on my shoulder and let it rest there for a while, so that I felt it warmer and warmer through the cotton of my shirt. I sensed then that she did love me in a way that wouldn't change, whatever her mood might be.

That fall, after the summer when they both died, she and my father, there was a point when I wanted to say to them, All right, you have died, I know that, and you've been dead for a while, we have all absorbed this and we've explored the feelings we had at first, in reaction to it, surprising feelings, some of them, and the feelings we're having now that a few months have gone by—but now it's time for you to come back. You have been away long enough.

Because after the dramas of the deaths themselves, those complicated dramas that went on for days, for both of them, there was the quieter and simpler fact of missing them. He would not be there to come out of his room at home with a picture or a letter to show us, he would not be there to tell us the same stories over again, about when he was a young boy—pronouncing the names that meant so much to him and so little to us: Clinton Street where he was born, Winter Island where they went in the summers when he was little, him watching the back of the horse that trotted ahead of them pulling their carriage, his pneumonia when he was a child, weakened and lying in bed reading, day after day, in that cousin's house in Salem, going to the Y on Saturdays to swim with the other boys, where it was the usual thing for all the boys to swim naked, and how that bothered him, the Perkins family next door. He would not be there having his first cup of coffee in the morning at eleven o'clock, or reading by the light from the window in an armchair. She would not be making pancakes for us in the mornings at the rented beach house, wide fat blueberry pancakes a little underdone in the middle, standing over the pan, quiet and concentrating, or talking as she worked, in her flowered blouse and straight pants, in her comfortable flats or her moccasins, the familiar shape of her toes in them stretching the fabric or the leather. She would not go out swimming in the rough waves of the harbor, even in stormy weather, her eyes a lighter blue than the water. She would not stand with our mother waist-deep in the water near the shore talking, with a little frown on her face either from the sunlight or from concentrating on what they were talking about. She would never again make oyster stew the way she did one Christmas Eve, on that visit to our mother and father's house after her husband died, the crunch of sand in our mouths in the milky broth, sand in the bottoms of our spoons. She would not take a child on her lap, her own child, as on that same visit, when they were all so sad and confused, or someone else's child, and rock that child quietly back and forth, her broad strong arms around the child's chest, resting her cheek against the child's hair, her face sad and thoughtful, her eyes distant. She would not be there on the sofa in the evenings, exclaiming in surprise when she saw an actor she knew in a movie or a show, she would not fall asleep there, suddenly quiet, later in the evening.

The first New Year after they died felt like another betrayal—we were leaving behind the last year in which they had lived, a year they had known, and starting on a year that they would never experience.

There was also some confusion in my mind, in the months afterwards. It was not that I thought she was still alive. But at the same time I couldn't believe that she was actually gone. Suddenly the choice wasn't so simple: either alive or not alive. It was as though not being alive did not have to mean she was dead, as though there were some third possibility.

Her visit, that time—now I don't know why it seemed so complicated. You just go out and do something together, or sit and talk if you stay inside. Talking would have been easy enough, since she liked to talk. Of course it's too simple to say that she liked to talk. There was something frantic about the way she talked. As though she were afraid of something, fending something off. After she died, that was one thing we all said—we used to wish she would stop talking for a while, or talk a little less, but now we would have given anything to hear her voice.

I wanted to talk, too, I had things to say in answer to her, but it wasn't possible, or it was difficult. She wouldn't let me, or I would have to force my way into the conversation.

I wish I could try again—I wish she would come and visit again. I think I would be calmer. I'd be so glad to see her. But it doesn't work that way. If she came back, she'd be back for more than just a little while, and maybe I wouldn't know what to do, after all, any better than the last time I saw her. Still, I'd like to try.

Another present was a board game involving endangered species. A board game—there was that optimism again. Or she was doing what our mother used to do—giving me something that required another person, so that I would have to bring another person into my life. I actually meet plenty of people, I even meet them traveling. Most people are basically pretty friendly. It's true that I still live alone, I'm just more comfortable that way, I like having everything the way I want it. But having a board game wasn't going to encourage me to bring someone home to play it with me.

There aren't that many of us in the car, though more than I would have expected on this particular day. Of course I think they're all on their way to some place that's welcoming and friendly, where people are waiting for them with things to eat and drink, like little sausages and eggnog. But that may not be true. And they may be thinking the same thing about me—if they are thinking anything about me.

And some of them who may not be going anywhere special may be glad, though that's a little hard to believe, because you're made to feel, by all the hype, by all the advertising, really, but also by the things your friends say, that you should be somewhere special, with your family, or with your friends. If you're not, you get that old feeling of being left out, another feeling you learned when you were a child, in school probably, at the same time that you learned to get excited seeing all those wrapped presents, no matter what you eventually found in them, besides what you wanted.

I'm not as cheerful as I used to be, I know. A friend of mine said something about it, after I lost both of them, three weeks apart, that summer: he said, your grief spreads into all sorts of different areas of your life. Your grief turns into depression. And after a while you just don't want to do anything. You just can't be bothered.

Another friend—when I told him, he said, "I didn't know you had a sister." So strange. By the time he found out I had a sister, I no longer had a sister.

It's beginning to rain, little drops driven sideways across the windowpane. Streaks and dots across the glass. The sky outside is darker and the lights in the car, the ceiling light and the little reading lights over the seats, seem brighter. The farms are passing now. There's no wash hanging out, but I can see the clotheslines stretched between the back porches and the barns. The farms are on both sides of the tracks, there are wide-open spaces between them, the silos far apart over the landscape, with the farm buildings clustered around them, like churches in their little villages in the distance.

Sometimes the grief was nearby, waiting, just barely held back, and I could ignore it for a while. But at other times it was like a cup that was always full and kept spilling over.

For a while, it was hard for me to think or speak about one of them separate from the other. For a while, though not anymore, they were always linked together in my mind because they died so close to each other in time. It was hard not to imagine her waiting for him somewhere, and him coming. We were even comforted by it—we imagined that she would take care of him, wherever they were. She was younger and more alert than he was. She was taller and stronger. But would he be pleased, or would he be annoyed? Would he want to be by himself?

I didn't even know if he wanted me to stay there next to the bed while he was dying. I had taken the bus to the city where he and my mother lived, to be with him. There would be no chance of recovery, for him, or going back from where he was, because they had stopped feeding him. He wasn't speaking or hearing, or even seeing, anymore, so there was no way to know what he wanted. He didn't look like himself. His eyes were half open, but they didn't see anything. His mouth was half open. He didn't have his teeth in. Once, I put a little wet sponge to his lower lip, because of the dryness, and his mouth clamped shut on it suddenly.

You think you should sit with someone who is dying, you think it must be a comfort to them. But when he was alive, when we lingered at the dinner table, or in the living room talking and laughing, after a while he always got up and left us and went into his own room. Later, when he was doing the dishes, he would say no, he didn't want any help. Even when we were visiting him in the nursing home, after an hour or two he would ask us to leave.

Our mother consulted a psychic, later, after they were gone, to see if she could get in touch with them. She didn't really believe in that sort of thing, but some friend of hers had recommended this psychic and she thought it might be interesting and couldn't hurt to try, so she met with her and told her things about them, and let her try to communicate with them.

The woman said she reached both of them. Our father was agreeable and cooperative, though he didn't say much, something noncommittal, that he was "all right." My mother thought that after the trouble they had gone to, to reach him, he might have said more. But our sister turned away and was cross, and didn't want to have anything to do with it. We were very interested in this, even though we had trouble believing it. We felt that at least the psychic believed it and thought she had had that experience.

The two kinds of grief were different. One kind, for him, was for an end that came at the right time, that was in the natural order of things. The other kind of grief, for her, was for an end that came unexpectedly and much too soon. She and I were just beginning a good correspondence—now it will never continue. She was just beginning a project of her own that meant a lot to her. She had just rented a house near us where we would be able to see her much more often. A different phase of her life was just beginning.

•

Strange, the way things look when you're watching them out a train window. I don't get tired of that. Just now I saw an island in the river, a small one with a grove of trees on it, and I was going to look more carefully at it, because I like islands, but then I looked away for a moment and when I looked back it was gone. Now we're passing some woods again. Now the woods are gone and I can see the river again and the hills in the distance. The things close to the tracks flash by so fast, and the things in the middle distance flow past more quietly and steadily, and the things in the far distance stay still, or some-times they seem to be moving forward, just because the things in the middle distance are moving backward.

Actually, even though things in the far distance seem to be staying still, or even moving forward a little, they are moving back very slowly. Those treetops on a hill in the far distance were even with us for a while, but when I looked again, they were behind us, though not far behind.

I kept noticing things, in the days after she died and then after he died: a white bird flying up seemed to mean something, or a white bird landing nearby. Three crows on the branch of a tree meant something. Three days after he died, I woke up from a dream about Elysian fields, as though he had now gone into them, as though he had hovered near us for a while, for three days, even floating over our mother's living room, and had then gone on, into the Elysian fields, maybe before going farther, to whatever place he was going to go and stay.

I wanted to believe all this, I tried hard to believe it. After all, we don't know what happens. It's such a strange thing— that once you are dead, you do know the answer, if you know anything at all. But whatever the answer is, you can't commu-nicate it to the ones who are still alive. And before you die, you can't know whether we live on in some form after we die, or just come to an end.

It's like what that woman in the store said to me the other day. We were talking about the little expressions our mothers liked to use over and over again—"To each his own," or "They meant well." She said her mother was Christian, and devout, and that she believed in an afterlife of the soul. But this woman herself did not believe, and would gently make fun of her mother. And whenever that happened, her mother would say to her, with a good-humored smile: When we die, one of us is going to be very surprised!

Our father himself believed that it was all in the body, and specifically in the brain, that it was all physical—the mind, the soul, our feelings. He had once seen a man's brains spread over the asphalt of a driveway after an accident. He had stopped his car on the street and got out to look. My sister was a little girl then. He told her to wait for him in the car. When the body was no longer alive, he said, it was all over. But I wasn't so sure.

There was the terror I felt one night as I was going to sleep—the sudden question that woke me up. Where was she going now? I sensed very strongly that she was going somewhere or had gone somewhere, not that she had simply stopped existing. That she, like him, had stayed nearby for a while, and then she was going—down, maybe, but also out somewhere, as though out to sea.

First, while she was still alive, but dying, I kept wondering what was happening to her. I did not hear much about it. One thing they said was that when her reflexes were worse, according to the doctors, she would move towards the pinch or the prick instead of away from it. I thought that meant that her body wanted the pain, that she wanted to feel something. I thought it meant she wanted to stay alive.

There was also that slow, dark dream I had about five days after her death. I may have had the dream just as her funeral was taking place, or just after. In the dream, I was making my way down from one level to the next in a kind of arena, the levels were wider and deeper than steps, down into a large, deep, high-ceilinged, ornately furnished and decorated room, or hall—I had an impression of dark furniture, sumptuous ornamentation, it was a hall intended for ceremony, not for any daily use. I was holding a small lantern that fit tightly over my thumb and extended outward, with a tiny flame burning in it. This was the only illumination in the vast place, a flame that wavered and flickered and had already gone out or nearly gone out once or twice. I was afraid that as I went down, as I climbed down with such difficulty, over levels that were too wide and deep to be easily straddled, the light would go out and I would be left in that deep well of darkness, that dark hall. The door I had come in by was far above me, and if I called out, no one would hear me. Without a light, I would not be able to climb back up those difficult levels.

I later realized that, given the day and the hour when I woke up from the dream, it was quite possible that I dreamt it just at the time she was being cremated. The cremation was to begin right after the funeral, my brother told me, and he told me when the funeral had ended. I thought the flickering light was her life, as she held on to it those last few days. The difficult levels descending into the hall must have been the stages of her decline, day by day. The vast and ornate hall might have been death itself, in all its ceremony, as it lay ahead, or below.

The odd problem we had afterwards was whether or not to tell our father. Our father was vague in his mind, by then, and puzzled by many things. We would wheel him up and down the hallway of his nursing home. He liked to greet the other residents with a smile and a nod. We would stop in front of the door to his room. In June, the last year he was alive, he looked at the Happy Birthday sign on the door and waved at it with his long, pale, freckled hand and asked me a question about it. He couldn't articulate his words very well anymore. Unless you had heard him all your life, you wouldn't know what he was saying. He was marveling over the sign, and smiling. He was probably wondering how they knew when his birthday was.

He still recognized us, but there was a lot he didn't understand. He was not going to live much longer, though we didn't know then how little time was left. It seemed to us important for him to know that she had died—his daughter, though she was really his stepdaughter. And yet, would he understand, if we told him? And wouldn't it only distress him terribly, if he did understand? Or maybe he would have both reactions at once—he might understand some part of what we were saying, and then feel terrible distress at both what we had told him and his inability to understand it completely. Should his last days be filled with this distress and grief?

But the alternative seemed wrong, too—that he should end his life not knowing this important thing, that his daughter had died. Wrong that he, who had once been the head of our small family, the one who, with our mother, made the most important family decisions, the one who drove the car when we went out on a little excursion, who helped our sister with her homework when she was a teenager, who walked her to school every morning when she was in her first year of school, while our mother rested or worked, who refused or gave permission, who played jokes at the dinner table that made her and her little friends laugh, who was busy out in the backyard for a few weeks building a playhouse—that he should not be shown the respect of being told that such an important thing had happened in his own family.

He had so little time left, and we were the ones deciding something about the end of his life—that he would die knowing or not knowing. And now I'm not sure what we did, it was so many years ago. Which probably means that nothing very dramatic happened. Maybe we did tell him, out of a sense of duty, but hastily, and nervously, not wanting him to understand, and maybe there was a look of incomprehension on his face, because something was going by too quickly. But I don't know if I'm remembering that or making it up.

On one of her visits to me, she gave me a red sweater, a red skirt, and a round clay tile for baking bread. She took a picture of me wearing the red sweater and the skirt. I think the last thing she gave me was those little white seals with perforated backs. They're filled with charcoal, which is supposed to absorb odors. You put them in your refrigerator. I guess she thought that because I live alone, my refrigerator would be neglected and smell bad, or maybe she just thought that anyone might need this.

When did she leave the tartar sauce? You wouldn't think a person could become attached to something like a jar of tartar sauce. But I guess you can—I didn't want to throw it out, because she had left it. Throwing it out would mean that the days had passed, time had moved on and left her behind. Just as it was hard for me to see the new month begin, the month of July, because she would never experience that new month. Then the month of August came, and he was gone by then, too.

Well, the little seals are useful to me, at least they were seven years ago. I did put them in my refrigerator, though at the back of a shelf, where I wouldn't have to look at their cheerful little faces and black eyes every time I opened the door. I even took them with me when I moved.

I doubt if they absorb anything anymore, after all this time. But they don't take up much room, and there isn't much in there anyway. I like having them, because they remind me of her. If I bend down and move things around, I can see them lying back there under the light that shines through some dried spilled things on the shelf above. There are two of them. They have black smiles painted on their faces. Or at least a line painted on their faces that looks like a smile.

Really, the only present I ever wanted, after I grew up, was something for work, like a reference book. Or something old.

Now there's a lot of noise coming from the café car—people laughing. They sell alcohol there. I've never bought a drink on a train—I like to drink, but not here. Our brother used to have a drink on the train sometimes, on his way home from seeing our mother. He told me that once. This year he's in Acapulco—he likes Mexico.

We have a couple of hours to go, still. It's dark out. I'm glad it was light when we passed the farms. Maybe there's a big family in the café car, or a group traveling to a conference. I see that all the time. Or to a sporting event. Well, that doesn't actually make much sense, not today. Now someone's coming this way, staring at me. She's smiling a little—but she looks embarrassed. Now what? She's lurching. Oh, a party. It's a party—in the café car, she tells me. Everyone's invited.

Learning Medieval History

Are the Saracens the Ottomans?
No, the Saracens are the Moors.
The Ottomans are the Turks.

My School Friend

story from Flaubert

Last Sunday I went to the Botanical Gardens. There, in the Trianon Park, is where that strange Englishman Calvert used to live. He grew roses and shipped them to England. He had a collection of rare dahlias. He also had a daughter who used to fool around with an old schoolmate of mine named Barbelet. Because of her, Barbelet killed himself. He was seventeen. He shot himself with a pistol. I walked across a sandy stretch of ground in the high wind, and I saw Calvert's house, where the daughter used to live. Where is she now? They've put up a greenhouse near it, with palm trees, and a lecture hall where gardeners can learn about budding, grafting, pruning, and training—everything they need to know to maintain a fruit tree! Who thinks about Barbelet anymore—so in love with that English girl? Who remembers my passionate friend?

The Piano Lesson

I am with my friend Christine. I have not seen her for a long time, perhaps seventeen years. We talk about music and we agree that when we meet again she will give me a piano lesson. In preparation for the lesson, she says, I must select, and then study, one Baroque piece, one Classical, one Romantic, and one Modern. I am impressed by her seriousness and by the difficulty of the assignment. I am ready to do it. We will have the lesson in one year, she says. She will come to my house. But then, later, she tells me she's not sure she will be returning to this country. Maybe, instead, we will have the lesson in Italy. Or if not Italy, then, of course, Casablanca.

dream

The Schoolchildren in the
Large Building

I live in a very large building, the size of a warehouse or an opera house. I am there alone. Now some schoolchildren arrive. I see their quick little legs coming through the front door and I ask, in some fear, "Who is it, who is it?" They don't answer. The class is very large—all boys, with two teachers. They pour into the painting studio at the back of the building. The ceiling of this studio is two or even three stories high. On one wall is a mural of dark-complexioned faces. The schoolboys crowd in front of the painting, fascinated, pointing and talking. On the opposite wall is another mural, of green and blue flowers. Only a handful of boys are looking at this one.

The class would like to spend the night here because they do not have funds for a hotel. Wouldn't their hometown raise the money for this field trip? I ask one of the teachers. No, he says sadly, with a smile, they wouldn't because of the fact that he, the teacher, is homosexual. After saying this, he turns and gently puts his arms around the other teacher.

Later, I am in the same building with the schoolchildren, but it is no longer my home, or I am not familiar with it. I ask a boy where the bathrooms are, and he shows me one—it's a nice bathroom, with old fixtures and paneled in wood. As I sit on the toilet, the room rises—because it is also an elevator. I wonder briefly, as I flush, how the plumbing works in that case, and then assume it has been figured out.

dream

The Sentence and the Young Man

A sentence lies exposed to public view, in an open trash can. It is the ungrammatical sentence "Who sing!?!" We are watching it from where we stand concealed in a shadowed archway. We see a young man walk past the trash can several times, eyeing the sentence curiously. We will stay where we are, for fear that, at any moment, he will reach in quickly and fix it.

dream

Molly, Female Cat: History/Findings

Description: spayed female, calico
History:
    Found in early spring at roadside curled up against snow-bank
    Age at time of adoption: approx. 3 yrs
    Likely abandoned by previous owners
    Confined to bathroom during first week
    Would not eat for one week in new home, but played actively in confined space
Skin/coat: Inflamed/irritated around neck
Parasites: flea dirt found
    Allowed to run free outdoors after adoption
    Keeps owners company in vegetable garden
Nose/Throat: no visible lesions
    Eating well, dry food
    Hunts small birds, but was not able to retain grip on large blue jay
Broken tooth: upper right canine
Dental disease grade: 2–3 out of 5
    Two other cats in house and they all run around in large house
    Will not play with other cats
Eyes: no visible lesions
Lungs: within normal limits

Will not play with owners in presence of other cats, but will play with owners in bathroom

Lymph nodes: normal

Heart: within normal limits

Affectionate with owners, purrs and closes eyes when petted

Hangs limp in owners' arms when picked up

Urogenital system: within normal limits

Urinates inappropriately at home on floor in 2–3 places per day

Getting worse over time, larger puddles of urine

Ears: no visible lesions

Moderate fascial skin restriction over lumbar back, significant over sacrum

Cries when petted just above tail

Sometimes cries before or after urinating

Sometimes cries after nap

Abdomen: no palpable lesions

Nervous system: within normal limits

Weight: 8.75 lbs

Ideal weight: 8.75 lbs

Does not use litter box—defecates on floor in vicinity of litter box

May have fleas

Pain score: 3 out of 10 (over sacrum)

Tolerates exam by vet, nervous but no overt hostility

Pulse: 180

Overall body condition score: 3 out of 5

Update:

Was urinating in larger quantities on floor when indoors

Chose to go outdoors every day despite adverse weather conditions

Could not be found at midday on very hot spring day
Was found in late afternoon under pine tree, panting and covered with flies
Was brought indoors and laid in cool shower stall
Stopped panting, resumed normal respiration
Died within several hours
Age at time of death: approx. 11 yrs

The Letter to the Foundation

Dear Frank and Members of the Foundation,

I was not able to finish this letter before now even though I began writing to you in my head immediately after your momentous phone call of September 29 all those many years ago. I was aware, in the first few days, of certain instructions you had given me—that I could tell the news to only two people, that I should be friendly to a college reporter, if one should approach me, that I should call you Frank. I did not think of sitting down and writing to you, because you had not specifically instructed me to do that.

I think you did say you were curious about what it was like to receive this grant, but by now I may be confusing something you said with something another person said to me, asking if I would describe for him what it was like. In any case, whether or not you asked me to describe it, I will do that.

I told you right away, Frank, that I wanted to write you a letter of thanks. You told me I really didn't have to. I said I wanted to, though. You laughed and said, Yes, you are a scholar and a teacher of literature, so you probably have a lot to say.

The trouble is, I am an honest and truthful person and I'm not sure how truthful I can be in writing to the Foundation. I don't want to tell you things you don't want to hear, after all. For instance, I don't think you want to hear that I didn't intend to work all the time during the period of the grant.

What happened first was that I did not believe I had been given this grant. For a surprisingly long time, I didn't believe it. I was so used to not receiving this grant. I knew about it. Our department at the college calls it the two-year grant. Other scholars I knew had gotten it. I had wanted it for many years. I had watched others receive it while I did not receive it: I was simply one of the hundreds and hundreds of scholars who ardently want one of these grants in order to be rescued at least temporarily from the life or the work they are subjected to— the heavy course load, the constant exhaustion, the annoying dean of studies or the impossibly detail-oriented acting chairwoman, the committee work, the endless office hours, the flickering fluorescent light in the office, the stains on the classroom carpeting, etc. I was deeply accustomed to being one of those who were passed over by the Foundation, who were rejected, who, in the eyes of the Foundation, should not receive this award and were less worthy than certain others. I therefore did not really believe I was one of those who had been rescued, or I was very slow to begin believing it, with the help of reminders that also seemed unreal after a while: "Good for you!" one of my colleagues would say. "What are your plans now?"

I was like an amnesiac who accepts what she is told about her life but does not remember any of it herself. Since she can't remember any of it, she can't deeply believe it, but she must accept it and become accustomed to it because so many people tell her the same facts over and over.

I will try to reconstruct the experience for you, since you asked.

It was just after nine in the morning when the Foundation telephoned.

I was getting ready to go into the city. I stopped what I was doing and talked to you. For a moment, I thought you might be calling for another reason. But at the same time, I was thinking that you wouldn't telephone me at nine in the morning for anything else—you would have written me a letter. The first person I talked to was a shy, gentle woman with a quiet voice. She gave me the good news and then told me that I should call another person from the Foundation right away, a man who might or might not be in his office.

Meanwhile, even as I was talking to her and hearing the good news, I was worried that I would miss my bus. I could not miss the bus because I had an appointment down in the city to the south of where I lived. I called the other person, the man, and he was in his office, which was a relief. I think this man was probably you, although by now, all these years later, I'm not sure. He began to tease me. He tried to make me think I had misunderstood what the gentle woman had said, and that I was not really going to be getting any grant. He must have known that I would be aware that he was teasing me, and he must have known, too, that I would be surprised that he was teasing me, and even worried about it, though I didn't know exactly in what way I should be worried. I wondered later if I was the only one you teased when talking about the good news, but since I can't believe that, I have to believe you make a habit of teasing the people you call—if it was you, of course.

I talked to him, or you, as long as you seemed to want me to talk. It was then that you gave me instructions. You told me to call you Frank. At that moment, I was prepared to do anything you seemed to want me to do, because I was afraid that if I was not careful at that moment, everything would be ruined and the grant would vanish. This was an instinctive reaction, not a rational one. When the conversation was over, I hurried to the bus.

I was glad, of course—I thought about the good news all the way in to the city. For the first time, also, I could observe exactly how my mind adapted to a suddenly new situation: over and over again, I caught myself thinking about something in the usual way and then told myself, No, now things are different. When this had happened enough times, at last my mind began to adapt to the new situation.

Later that day, I was having lunch by myself in a restaurant near the public library. I ordered a half sandwich and a cup of soup, which cost about $7. After the waitress walked away, I continued to think about the menu, because, really, I would have preferred a certain favorite salad for $11. Then I realized: I could have afforded the salad! But immediately afterwards I thought, No! Be careful! If you spend half again as much as you used to spend on each thing that you buy from now on, you will soon run out of money!

I was feeling such relief. I wanted to tell the Foundation about this immense relief. But then I thought that of course it must be obvious to you. You probably hear this from every person you help. Does every person let you know? Or are some people very quiet or very matter-of-fact? Are they very pragmatic, and do they immediately plan how they will put it to use? Are some people not even relieved, though they are happy and excited? Or not even happy and excited? Still, I wanted to tell the Foundation. I wanted to tell you that now everything was going to be all right—I would not have to worry.

I wanted to tell you that during all of my adult life, starting at the age of twenty-one, I had worried about how I would earn enough to live on for the next year, sometimes for the next week. When I was still young, and even when I was older, my parents sometimes sent me small sums of money to help out, but the burden was on me, it was my responsibility, I knew that, and my next year's income was never secure. Sometimes I was frightened because I had so little money and did not see how I could earn more. The fear would be something I felt physically in the pit of my stomach. It would come upon me suddenly:

What was I going to do? Once, I had no money at all except for the $13 that a friend owed me. I did not want to ask her to pay it back, but I did. Most of all, I wanted to tell you that now I would not have to do the work I was doing that was so difficult for me. By that, I meant teaching.

Teaching has always been so difficult. At times, it has been a disaster. I'm not afraid of hard work, and I'm used to it, but this particular kind of work, the kind of teaching I do, has been crushing and almost debilitating. Particularly difficult was the year before I received that telephone call, and also the year in which I received it. In those days, I wanted to cry, I wanted to shout, I wanted to wring my hands and complain, and I did try to complain to some people, though I could never cry or complain as much as I wanted to. Some people listened and tried to be helpful, but they could never listen long enough; the conversation always had to come to an end. I always kept most of my emotion to myself. I was still in the midst of teaching then, when the Foundation called, but with the great difference, after the call, that I thought I wouldn't be continuing. I had two more months of it, I thought, and then I would be done with it, maybe forever.

I have so often sat on the bus traveling up to the college, on those mornings, wishing something would come down and rescue me, or that there would be a minor accident, one in which no one was hurt, or at least not badly hurt, that would prevent me from teaching the class.

That is how the teaching day begins. I take a public bus from my town to the small city one hour north, where the college is. I do not drive my car, even though I could. I do not want that extra responsibility on a teaching day. I don't want to have to think about steering the car.

I sit there quietly in the bus looking out the window. The

bus rolls me gently from side to side and presses me back into the seat when it accelerates, or drops out from under me briefly when it goes over a bump. I like the way the bus rolls me around. I do not like the song that goes through my head. It always goes through my head for a while before I notice it. It is not a song of celebration. It is a dull and repetitious song that is often in my head, and I don't know why: it is "The Mexican Hat Dance."

I also wanted to tell you how I was running out of money when this news came. I had less in my bank account than I had had in years, though some small jobs would be coming in the spring. Now at last I would have enough money, thanks to you, if I didn't die first.

There would be enough to live on, and there would even be extra money I could spend on things I wanted or needed. I could buy a new pair of glasses, maybe more attractive ones, though that is always difficult. I could have more expensive food for dinner. But as soon as I began to think of what I might buy with the extra money, I was either ashamed or embarrassed—because although new glasses and a better dinner would be nice, they were not really necessary, and exactly how many things should I allow myself to buy that are not really necessary?

Now a strange thing was happening. I sometimes felt removed from my life, as though I were floating above it or maybe a little to the side of it. This sensation of floating must have come from the fact that I thought I would no longer be attached to anything, or to much: I thought I would not be attached to my teaching job, and I thought I would not be attached by those many strings to all the necessary other small and large jobs that would earn me four thousand dollars, or three, or two, to cover three months, or two, or one. I was floating up and looking out over a longer distance, at more of the landscape in a circle around me.

The department gave a little party to congratulate me on

the grant. It is not such a large grant, but the department likes to make a fuss over anything that its faculty does. It wants the college administration to know about the faculty's accomplishments and to think well of the department. But this party made me uncomfortable. The department, and maybe the college, too, now valued me more than they had before, and at the same time I now wanted to leave the college. In fact, I was secretly planning to leave it. I would either cut my ties completely or have as little to do with it as possible.

It turned out that I could not stop teaching. But I did not know that for a while.

I am not always a bad teacher. My difficulty teaching is complex, and I've given it a lot of thought: it is probably due to a general lack of organization on my part, to begin with, combined with overpreparation, then stage fright, and, in the classroom itself, poor articulation of ideas and a weak classroom presence. I have trouble looking the students in the eye. I mumble or fail to explain things clearly. I do not like to use the blackboard.

I do not like to use the blackboard because I do not like to turn my back on the class. I'm afraid that if I do, the students will take advantage of this to talk to one another or review notes from another course, or worse, they will stare at the back of me, and certainly not with admiration. All of last year I did not use the blackboard. This year I began to use it. When I do use it, I am so hasty and uncomfortable, and my handwriting is so poor, that the words I write are small and faint and hard to read.

This is the way I work: I avoid the thought of the class as long as I can. Then, when there is not much time left, maybe a day or an evening, I begin to prepare it. In preparing it, unfortunately, I also begin to imagine it. In imagining it, I become so afraid of the classroom and the students that I freeze and can no longer think clearly. Sometimes I am able to control my panic—suppress it or talk myself out of it—and then, for minutes at a time, even half an hour, I am able to plan the class in a reasonable way. Then the panic sets in again and I can't think anymore. Every plan seems wrong, I believe that I know nothing, I have nothing to teach. And the more trouble I have planning, the more frightened I become, because time is passing and the hour for the class is drawing closer.

The feeling I mentioned, of being removed from my life, was like what I imagine a person feels who learns she has a fatal illness. There was also a greater clarity of vision—which may also come when one is dying. It seemed that it wasn't I who had changed but everything around me. Everything was sharper, clearer, and closer, as though, before, I had been seeing only little bits at a time, not all of it, or all of it but veiled or clouded. What was blocking my view before? Was there a veil between me and the world, or did I have blinkers on that narrowed my vision and kept me looking ahead? I did not know this until now—that I must have had a habit of not looking all around me. It was not that I had taken everything for granted before, but that I could not look at everything at once. Why? Was it so that I would not be tempted to do what I did not have the time or money to do, or so that I would not even think about something too distracting? I had to ignore so much of the world, or turn my thoughts away from it and back to the business at hand, whatever that might be. I could not let my thoughts go wherever they wished to and then on to something else.

Now everything looked different—as if I had returned to earth and were looking at it again. Was each thing more beautiful? No, not exactly. Perhaps more completely itself, more full, more vital. Was this the way things looked to people who had come back to life from a near-death experience?

I already knew that I had the habit of looking out from the

window of a car or bus with longing at certain things in the distance that I would never visit, that I would wish to visit but that I would not visit—in one place I lived, it was an old, run-down California ranch house in a stand of eucalyptus and palm trees across an overgrown field. A long, curving dirt driveway led up to it.

From the bus on the way up to the college these days I see something rather similar: an old farmhouse with outbuildings, with trees around it and a field between the highway and the house. It is a very simple, old frame house, and the trees are a simple group of tall shade trees.

I used to think these places had to remain at just this distance, that I should long for them and that they should be almost imaginary, and that I should never visit them. Now, for a while, feeling as though I were outside my life, I thought I could visit them.

At the same time, I felt closer to strangers. It was as though something had been taken away that used to stand between me and them. I don't know if this was connected with the feeling that I was not inside my own life anymore. I suppose by "my own life" I mean the habitual worries, plans, and constraints that I thought were no longer even relevant. I noticed this feeling of closeness to strangers most of all in the bus station, which is where I see many strangers all at once in a crowd and watch them for as long as an hour or two at a time, for instance when I am waiting for the late-night bus home and I sit in the cafeteria writing a letter or reading student papers.

I have to say that once the class is under way, the tension is not nearly as bad as during the hours leading up to it and particularly those last ten or twenty minutes just before it. The worst moment of all is the last moment, in my office, in which I get up from my chair, pick up my briefcase, and open the office door. Even five minutes, the five minutes remaining before I have to walk out of my office, are enough to give me a little feeling of protection, although that five minutes is almost too short a period of time to be of any use. But ten minutes is certainly long enough to protect me from that last minute.

I should know by now that once it begins, the hour itself will not be as bad as those ten or twenty minutes before it, and especially that last minute. If I really knew that the hour itself would not be as bad, then I wouldn't be so afraid of it, and then of course those ten or twenty minutes beforehand would not be so bad. But there seems to be no way, yet, to convince myself of that. And, of course, sometimes it really is very bad.

Once, for instance, the class discussion got out of hand and offensive remarks were made by some of the students against certain groups of people, remarks which, since I did not know how to stop them quickly, may have appeared to have been made with my approval or even encouragement. Some of the other students, and I myself, became increasingly uncomfortable as the discussion continued. A more adept teacher could have broadened the discussion and rescued it, for instance by turning it into a lesson on the subject of the dangers of generalizing versus its usefulness. But I was not able to think of any way to do that right there on the spot, and the class ended with a bad feeling. Later, at home, I had some good and smart things to say that would have helped, but it was too late. I dreaded the next class and the chill that would pervade it. And I was not mistaken about the next class.

It is not often that the discussion goes in an unfortunate direction. More often there are just moments of awkwardness. Sometimes I hesitate while speaking, for instance, not because I am about to seize upon the perfect phrase or image, but because I have lost my train of thought and need to find some conclusion for my remark that will make sense. When I hesitate, the students become particularly riveted. They are far more interested when I grope for what to say next than they are when I am speaking on and on smoothly. Then, the more intently they watch me, waiting to see what I will say next, the more I am at a loss for what to say. I am afraid of becoming completely paralyzed. I must playact, and hide the fact that I am nearly paralyzed, and push myself on to some conclusion, at least a temporary one. Then they lose interest.

But what I dread in the classroom is not just the bad moment that I can't rescue or the many awkward moments when I feel inadequate. It is something larger. I do not want to be the focus of attention of a large group of students who are waiting to see what I will do or say next. It is such an uneven match. There are so many on one side, in rows, staring at just one alone in front of them. My very face seems to change. It becomes more vulnerable, because it is not looked at charitably, as it would be by a friend or an acquaintance, or even a person on the other side of a counter from me in a store or a bank, but critically, as a sort of foreign object. The more bored the students are, the more my face and body become foreign objects to be examined critically. I know this because I have been a student myself.

It is true that the first meeting of the class is not as difficult for me as the ones that come after, because there is so much business to be done and I am perfectly competent to do it. I take attendance, and I explain the syllabus and what I will expect from them. I don't mind fumbling among my lists and Xeroxed handouts because most teachers do that on the first day. I adopt the pose of the competent teacher, and they believe me for the space of that first class. I am greatly helped by the fact that they have had so many teachers all their lives, competent teachers, or at least confident and powerful teachers—so I can play the part of a confident, even commanding teacher and they will believe it. I'm sometimes good at acting a part and I can convince them for a while.

There have even been good moments during a class. Sometimes the discussion is interesting and the students seem surprised and engaged. There has even been a rare class that is good from beginning to end. I do like the students—most of them anyway, though not all of them. I have always liked them, maybe because, since they depend on me to give them a good grade, they show me their best face and their sweetest nature.

I do enjoy reading what they write. Every week there is a fresh pile of writing, most of it neatly typed and presented, if nothing else, and I always expect to find some treasure in it. And there really is always something good in it, and occasionally something, an idea or at the very least a sentence or a phrase, that is very good. The most exciting moment is when a student who has not been particularly good suddenly does something very fine. In fact, reading the students' work and writing comments on it is my favorite part of teaching, partly because I am at home, alone, usually lying on my bed or on the sofa.

But these good times and the few successful classes are far outweighed by the difficult times.

When I first received the news of this grant, I dreamed that I might not only stop teaching but at last leave my study and enter public life. I even thought I might run for office, though not a very high office—the school board or the town planning board. Then I wondered if I would do anything public after all. Maybe I would just continue to spend most of my time by myself in my study. Or I would stay in my study, but from there I would write a column for the local newspaper.

Later I thought that maybe each stage of this reaction simply had to wear itself out, and at last I would return to some kind of normal condition. And maybe that was all I really wanted—to feel all the same things I was used to feeling, and to do the same things I was used to doing, the only difference being that

I had a little more time, and a little less work, and a slightly higher opinion of myself.

The college I myself had attended, my alma mater, had never been in touch with me after I graduated, not even to ask for news for the alumnae magazine or for money. Then, as soon as an announcement of the grant was printed in an academic bulletin, the president herself wrote to congratulate me. She told me that a letter would be sent inviting me to give a talk there in the spring. I waited, but received no letter. I wrote a note of inquiry and received no answer. After a few more months, my alma mater began writing to me again, but only to send the alumnae magazine and to ask for money.

Then at last I began to feel normal again. For weeks I had felt vaguely ill, and afraid of accidents. I was afraid I would die. Why was I immediately afraid I would die? Was my life suddenly worth more because of this grant? Or did I think that because something good had happened to me, now something bad was going to happen? Was I afraid I would not be able to enjoy this good fortune because I would die first? It had been promised to me, and they, or you, couldn't take it away. But you had been careful to say, in the very first letter you sent to me, that if I were to die, no one else, no one in my family, for instance, my mother or my sisters or my brother, could have it. What you didn't need to say was that if I died, of course, I couldn't have it either.

Or did I think that now that I had been promised something this good, I would die before I received it?

I had sudden generous impulses. I wanted to give money to my friends, and I wanted to give twenty-dollar bills to strangers in the city. I thought of donating something to the sad, shabby bus station, maybe some large plants and a shelf of books for the waiting area.

Then I was warned by a friend who had been through this before. She said to watch out: I would have an almost irresistible impulse to give all the money away.

There were many things I had wanted to do in my life and had never done because there was no time. I am not graceful, but I like to dance. I wanted to sing, even though my voice is thin and weak. But of course this award was not given to me for those things. The Foundation had not intended to support me during the time I spent dancing and singing.

I used to dream about the nice things I would buy if I had enough money. Now a combination of shame and caution stopped me from spending the money freely or foolishly. I did, though, sometimes think about what I wanted to buy. I had a list: I wanted a canoe, an old wardrobe, a better piano, a dining table, a small piece of land, a trailer to put on it, a fishpond, some farm animals, and a shed to keep them in. This was in addition to some nicer clothes.

I thought I had to be careful, though. If I bought something that was not necessary but that gave me pleasure, it might be expensive to keep, like the nice piece of land, on which I would have to pay taxes. Or it might require constant care, like the farm animals.

I never did buy any of those things.

After there was a notice in the college newspaper, I expected reactions and questions from the students at the next class. I was looking forward to the chance to talk to them about this exciting event. I wanted to talk to them about research, and how exciting it can be. I thought it would be easy to talk about this, and interesting, and it might increase their respect for me. I am much better in the classroom if I think they respect me. I prepared for this discussion, imagining their questions and thinking of some answers. But none of them had heard the news, and no one said anything about it. Since I had prepared for their interested questions and not for their blank silence, I was even stiffer and more awkward than usual.

Now I see why I have been writing to you so much about teaching. I did not dare tell myself, before, just how much it bothered me, because I had to live with it. Then I thought I would never have to teach again. That was when I could admit that it was the worst torture—to be placed in front of that audience of indifferent or even possibly mocking young students.

At first I thought my fear confronting the class was reasonable: what could be more terrifying than to stand up there in front of those ranks of critical or indifferent or contemptuous young people, exposed to their eyes and their thoughts in all my uncertainty, my unimpressive exterior, my lack of training, my lack of confidence and command. There was some truth to that. But I have done this over and over again at different schools for years now. Finally, at the start of that important year, the year of your phone call, when my fear had not lessened or vanished, as I thought it might, now that I had had some experience at this particular college, I had to face the fact that my fear was exaggerated and unnatural. Certain friends agreed with me.

For instance, on the very first day of classes the first year I taught at this college, I had what I now think was a psychosomatic injury, if that's the right term for an injury caused purely by an emotional condition: I woke up with a large blood clot in one eye. To myself, looking in the mirror, I seemed grotesque, monstrous. I don't know if, when I stood there confronting the class later that day, the students noticed this blood clot. Since of course they would not say anything to me about it, I never knew. And it is true that students of that age are in general more interested in their own business than in any teacher, with or without a blood clot in her eye.

Later in the term, I developed such a bad infection in the tip of one finger from an embedded sliver that I required surgery, and I wore a large bandage to class. The surgery left a permanent scar and indentation in that fingertip, and some loss of sensation. I can't help seeing this injury, too, as a pathetic attempt to disable myself so that I could not teach.

After the finger had healed and the bandage was off, I began falling asleep at odd times, for several minutes at a time. I fell asleep not only on the bus, which was not so surprising, but also in my office, with my head down on my desk or tipped back, and in my car, in parking lots after shopping, and lying in the dentist's chair, and sitting in a row with other patients in the office of the eye doctor, waiting for my eyes to dilate. Obviously, I must have thought that falling asleep was one way to avoid my situation for at least a little while.

During the whole term, I wore black—a black coat, black shoes, black pants, and a black sweater—as though it were some sort of protection. Black was certainly a strong color, and maybe I thought that appearing in black would convince the students that I was a strong person. I was supposed to lead them in a confident way. But I did not want to be their leader—I have never wanted to be anyone's leader.

When I wasn't expecting it anymore, the students began to find out about my award and to ask questions. They seemed really interested in the news. They seemed to enjoy the sudden minor campus celebrity of their teacher. The novelty, the break in routine, which I welcomed, probably relieved them, too. Whenever anything out of the ordinary takes place in the class, such as a sudden thunderstorm, or a blizzard, or an electrical outage, or my appearing with that large bandage on my finger, I relax a little and the hour goes better.

The teaching was almost over for the semester. The last class would meet in eight days.

I was feeling the approach of death, maybe because the time was coming when the Foundation would give me my first check. The only thing that could stop me from receiving the money in January was my own death. So I was thinking that the new year would inescapably bring either my death or the first check from the Foundation.

At the last class, we had a party of sorts, although I made them do some classwork first. I had carried two bottles of cider up on the bus in a backpack, along with a bag of good cider doughnuts. We arranged the chairs in a very large circle, although that was not my idea. I could not think how to conduct a party with twenty-five undergraduates. I did not think it would be very festive for them to sit in rows facing me and eating their messy doughnuts. But to move the chairs out of the way and mill around standing up, as at a cocktail party, also seemed awkward, since not all the students were friends with one another.

Now I was a little sorry to say goodbye to them. It was easier to miss them and think fondly of them when I didn't have to be afraid of them anymore.

Once the classes were over and the burden of teaching was taken away, of course I continued to teach in my own imagination, thinking of yet another reading assignment or smart comment. I imagined them all sitting there, receptive and interested, whereas actually they were by then sitting in other classes, or still on vacation, and not giving me or my course another thought, except maybe to wonder what their grade would be.

Soon after the new year, I met with a tax advisor, and he gave me some bad news. A large part of the grant would go to paying taxes—on the grant! Another part of it would have to be put away in a special account—to avoid being taxed. What was left would not be enough to live on. I realized that I would have to continue looking for small, temporary jobs in almost the same way I did before. But I still thought I would not have to teach.

Even at first, though, I had not wanted to cut my ties to the college completely. I thought I could give some lectures. I am not afraid of standing up in front of an audience to deliver a lecture that I have written ahead of time. I could do this in exchange for a small fee, I thought. But my plan to give lectures turned out to be impossible. I was told, instead, that I could receive a very small salary if I agreed to teach a special short course each fall, for people from the community. People from the community are usually older, sometimes quite old, and often eccentric. They are also more sympathetic and more respectful of a teacher, so I welcomed this solution.

Then I was no longer afraid of dying. Was this because I had already received some of the money? Was I thinking that if I died now, I would at least not have lost all of it? I had an idea that at first seemed unrelated to my fear of dying: I should prepare for my death now, so that this preparation would be "out of the way" and I could then carry on with my life. If death was the worst thing I had to fear, then I should make my peace with it. But in fact, how could I have thought that this feeling was not related to my earlier fear of dying?

I was also about to begin my letter to the Foundation, I thought. I would tell the Foundation that I was doing everything with more care. You would probably be happy to hear that. And I would tell you that, far from acquiring more things, as I could, now that I had a little more money, I wanted to get rid of all the things I didn't need, the things that had been stacked on top of bookcases and covered with a thick layer of sticky dust, or pushed inside cupboards, packed in boxes, or crowded into the back of a cabinet in the bathroom, mildewing.

Yet I knew that this might not interest you.

In the letter I was going to write to the Foundation, I was not sure I would tell them about my plans, although maybe I would explain that in my life as it was before, I did not have time for such things as stopping to talk to my neighbors. I was grateful to the Foundation that I could now do these things. I would not tell you that I was not yet working on any serious project, or that I presently spent my days sorting things: medications, lotions, and ointments; magazines and catalogues; socks, pens, and pencils. Maybe I was sorting things because I thought I was going to die. Or maybe I felt that I was not worthy of this award, and that if the Foundation could look in on my life for a few minutes, it would be appalled at the disorder.

I really didn't think the Foundation had this in mind when they awarded me the grant. I was afraid they would feel they had wasted their money. It would be too late for them to take it back, but they would be disappointed or even angry.

But perhaps my own conscience would sooner or later make me return to the work I should be doing. And perhaps the Foundation was relying on the fact that in the end my conscience would not let me waste my time and therefore their money.

After I received the first installment of the grant, I was wondering if I could buy something expensive. Then, one day, I nearly bought, by mistake, a sweater that cost $267. I think that is an expensive sweater, though some people would not think so, I know. I had misread the tag and thought it cost $167, which was already expensive enough. I had taken a deep breath and decided to buy it. I did not even try it on—I was afraid I would lose my nerve. When the salesgirl wrote up the slip, I saw the mistake and had to tell her that I would not buy it after all. It was a plain red cardigan. I did not really understand why the material and the one interesting design feature made it so much more expensive than what I was used to paying.

I continued to stand there by the cash register, probably in part so that the salesgirl would think I was not embarrassed at having changed my mind because of the price. I looked down into the glass case of jewelry and admired a necklace that cost $234. It was pretty, but not so pretty that I thought I should spend that amount of money on it. Then I asked the price of a gold bracelet, and she told me that it cost nearly $400. "Gold is expensive, after all," she said. It was a simple, delicate little bracelet with tiny, thin disks of gold strung on a piece of something I can't remember now. It was very pretty. But no matter how pretty it was, I would never have spent $400 for it or for any piece of jewelry. In the end, I bought only what I might have bought anyway, a pair of earrings for $36.

I didn't know if I should ever wear anything expensive. I thought I could, just once, buy one thing as expensive as that bracelet. But should I? I had at one time decided that I would own just a few clothes and that they would be simple but well made. I still had that idea. But if they were well made, did that also mean they were expensive? To dress simply was not necessarily enough if the simple clothes were very expensive. But then, maybe excellent quality would be all right if I bought the clothes secondhand. They would be secondhand, simple, old, a little worn, but of excellent quality. That seemed like a good compromise. But then I worried that if I shopped for them at a secondhand store, I would possibly be taking them away from someone else who really needed them.

I was going to be busy that spring. The spring had already been planned long before to include a number of rather tiresome short-term jobs that I could not cancel now, such as producing reader's reports for a publisher, writing short articles, and delivering papers at minor conferences. So my life did not feel any different, and did not seem any more free than it had been, except that from time to time I remembered that I would not be teaching in the fall—as I wrongly believed. The summer would come and I would really be free of every obligation.

But by the time the summer did come, with the prospect of that short course I was now going to have to teach, so many months had passed that I had grown used to feeling two contradictory things: that everything in my life had changed; and that, really, nothing in my life had changed.

This teaching, here at the college, was not even the first time I had ever taught, as I told you earlier. In other years, some classes went well and some badly. I can remember feeling so faint during the first meeting of one class that I had to put the students to work at an exercise that I contrived on the spot, while I left the room. I went to stand on an outdoor walkway and stared at a grove of eucalyptus trees until I felt better.

Another class, a few years later, at a different college, happened to meet in a room that had once been used as an office by a close friend of mine. In this very same room I had had a series of difficult encounters with her. Maybe that was what made the class particularly hard. During the first meeting, one talented student spoke up rudely when he found out what my requirements were for the course, and he dropped out immediately. I later offended another one because I said something personal which she took the wrong way.

My office hours were scheduled for the hour before the class. None of my students ever came to see me, not once, and so I always sat in my cubicle alone. It was an evening class, and the building was almost empty at that hour, but next door to me was another cubicle occupied by a more popular and successful teacher. I would sit alone in the nearly empty building and listen to everything he said to the steady stream of his own students.

I tell myself: There are just four of these hours each week. The four hours come one at a time, two on Tuesday and then two more on Thursday—just four small hours out of the whole week. But each casts a very long, very dark shadow on the day before, even on the two days before, and that shadow is especially dark the morning of each day of classes, and then darkest of all during those terrible ten or twenty minutes before the class, which include the last, almost unbearable minute of walking out the door of my office.

I also tell myself that many people in the world have awful jobs, and that compared to those jobs, this is a good job.

I have been writing to you at length about teaching. That is because when your grant came, I thought I wouldn't have to teach anymore. I also thought, and still think, that because you took enough interest in my work to give me the grant, you would be interested in everything about me and everything I had to say. I know this may not be true, but still I choose to believe that you care about how I am and what I am doing.

My mental habits are so fixed that I go on thinking the same things in the same way even when my circumstances have changed. But for a while, after the news, my vision of things widened. I saw more, on the peripheries, and I also observed and took pleasure in my wider vision itself. On one day, at least, I got into my car and drove into neighborhoods I had never explored before. I explored the new space, or the new time, that had been given to me. Then, maybe under the pressure of the various jobs in the spring, my vision narrowed again, I became intent on what I had to do, I concentrated on the next thing I had to do and not on my larger prospects. My vision led me only from breakfast to lunch and from lunch to dinner.

Then, when I finished all the work I was scheduled to do in the spring, a deep laziness set in, to my surprise. What began as a great relaxation, once the pressure was lifted, became an endless, boundless laziness in which I willfully refused to do most of what was asked of me unless the person asking was right there in front of me. Any request from a distance, any letter or any other communication, I simply ignored. Or I answered it quickly so as to make it go away. I said I was too busy to do whatever it was they wanted, too occupied. I was too occupied with doing nothing.

Usually I am a person of great energy. I can tackle any job, if asked, I can make myself do it, I can accomplish a whole string of tasks in succession at great speed and with great attention at the same time. Now, just when I was given such an opportunity to work on a project requiring research, for instance, all my energy deserted me suddenly, I was helpless, I said over and over again to anyone who asked me, "I'm sorry, I'm too busy, I have too much to do already."

No one could know, after all. Maybe I was really busy and maybe I wasn't. Sometimes I said, "Could you please ask me again in a year?" because some of them were friendly, good people and I did not want to disappoint them. I wanted to do whatever it was that they were asking, as long as I did not have to do it just then. I could certainly imagine having the will and the energy to do it at some point in the future.

I tried to think what the reason might be for this strange laziness. It might be this: I had been given something I did not have to earn, something other people considered important, but I did not feel very important myself. I had not felt very important before, and now this thing that I had been given had reduced me further. I was certainly much smaller and less important than what had been given to me. I was only a recipient, in this interaction. A recipient is not very active or important. The Foundation was active, giving me the money. It had changed my life for a while, with one decision and one phone call. I was active only to the extent of saying, Thank you! Thank you! After two years, the grant would be over. My gratitude would have been very active all that time—but would I have done anything?

Then some of my energy returned, and I was able to do some of what I had to do, though not much at a time—a single business letter on one day, and a single personal letter on another. I had not yet written the letter to the Foundation. I realize now that I was wrong to promise you a letter. You had not expected one, but because I promised one, you would now be expecting one, and you would now think that I was someone who did not do what she promised to do.

One day late in the summer that first year, I was riding the bus along the same route I always took to go to class. That day it happened to be the first part of a much longer trip that would take me far away, nowhere near the college. But I noticed, as I rode north on the bus, how the same misery closed around me, even though I was not on my way up to the college. How strange, I thought: the memory is still too vivid for me to be able to contemplate it calmly. The memory of that misery was itself too filled with misery—that misery was too close, as though it were still lying there in wait for me, as though I might slip over into that alternative reality at any moment.

It may be hard for you to believe that I find some small enjoyment in what comes before the class itself, just because it is not the class, just because I am not yet even on the campus. For instance, I take some satisfaction in the little stages of the trip itself: first the bus from my town north to that small city, then the city bus out to the college campus. The city bus costs me nothing if I show my college ID, and I enjoy this privilege more than you would think. To get from the first bus to the second, there is a brisk walk in the morning sunlight from the bus station over to the main downtown street. The walk lasts seven minutes, during which I pass a restaurant where, at that hour, an employee is always washing down the terrace and setting out the tables and chairs. After I pass this restaurant, I cross the wide main street and then turn left and walk uphill a few blocks to the city bus stop. This uphill walk is good for my heart, I always say to myself.

Before I pass the restaurant, I pass a travel agent, and of course the travel agent, combined with the restaurant, its outdoor tables and its early-morning activity, make me think of a foreign country, a place far away. I feel for just a moment as though I am far away, and that makes me wish even more that I were not here.

If I take the city bus a little later than usual, there is an extra stop on the route, and I prefer this route because it takes more time: the bus, after leaving the city limits, enters a large isolated office complex where the workers are often walking energetically around the looping sidewalks in pairs or alone. Very rarely does anyone get off or on the bus at this stop.

To comfort myself, I often think for just a moment of a certain great, strange, and difficult French poet who taught in a high school year after year because he had no other way to earn his living. Year after year, the students in the school made fun of him. Or at least that is what I remember reading somewhere.

The cafeteria in the bus station is where I spend the last part of my week, the evening before my late bus home. This evening is a peaceful time, perhaps the most peaceful of the week, filled with the enormous relief of having just finished the week of teaching and having before me the longest possible stretch of time before the next week begins, bringing with it the first class of the week.

I buy something, usually a cup of hot chocolate, in order to be able to sit down, and then I find a clean table, or I wash off a part of a table to make a clean place for my things. I settle down to read or correct papers. The tables in the cafeteria are ample and strong and well made, with smooth surfaces of a nice yellow hard plastic, with edges of light-colored laminated wood. I am perfectly happy with my cup of chocolate, my white napkin, and my book or my papers. Nothing is lacking in that interval of time. The two hours or so pass in perfect tranquillity, a tranquillity that would not be possible in a more complicated situation, one with more choices, for instance. There are noises all around me, but no noise bothers me. I listen to the staff of the cafeteria talk to one another and joke and laugh, and I feel that they are companions of a sort. I take comfort in the noises of the game machines that occupy one corner of the place, the most persistent noise being the solemn narrating voice that introduces the "18-Wheeler" game, the repeated horn blasts of the game's tractor-trailer; the thumps, cries, and metallic crashes of another game, like heavy swords clashing or infinitely repeated roadwork; and colliding with these noises, the young and enthusiastic recorded voice that introduces the "Sports-Shooting USA" game, along with the recorded roars of the crowds of spectators.

But when the next week begins and I make my way back up to the college, heading for the first class, I have to walk past that cafeteria, which was such a sanctuary at the end of the week before. I hear its familiar noises, the calls of the employees, the tinkle and bang and clash and recorded voices of the games. I hear them, not over and over again, as I do when I sit there in the evening with my hot chocolate, but only for a moment as I walk past the door with my briefcase. I might long to be inside the cafeteria, but I do not even dare admit that. Instead, I turn my thoughts away and walk on out of the station towards the main street and the city bus, as the noises of the cafeteria recede behind me. Since that sanctuary is not within my reach just then, it is no more valuable to me than if it had never been within my reach. In fact, since I can't enter it then, I would rather not see or hear it at all. And each time I go near it, I experience both feelings again, the relief and the dread, but the dread is stronger.

After a year had passed since I received the news, I wanted to return to what I thought of as my normal condition. I had to some extent returned to it, but I noticed that the normal condition included some of the old feelings of constraint. I did not feel the same freedom that I had felt in the beginning, soon after hearing the good news. I was worrying about time again, the way I always had. I would make schedules and more schedules. I recorded how long it took to do certain household tasks. I thought I would add up all the minutes it took to do certain necessary chores and calculate what was the least amount of time I needed to allow for this tedious work.

I had had a feeling of freedom because of the sudden change in my life. By comparison to what had come before, I felt immensely free. But then, once I became used to that freedom, even small tasks became more difficult. I placed constraints on myself, and filled the hours of the day. Or perhaps it was even more complicated than that. Sometimes I did exactly what I wanted to do all day—I lay on the sofa and read a book, or I typed up an old diary—and then the most terrifying sort of despair would descend on me: the very freedom I was enjoying seemed to say that what I did in my day was arbitrary, and that therefore my whole life and how I spent it was arbitrary.

This feeling of arbitrariness was similar to a feeling that had come over me after an incident some years before in a diner next door to another bus station. I hope you won't mind if I explain it. It does seem relevant, in some way, to what I experienced when the Foundation awarded me the two-year grant.

I was meeting a friend who was coming in on a bus. I was at the bus station. This was a different bus station, the one in my own hometown, not the station I have so often passed through on my way to the college. I was told that my friend's bus was going to be quite late. After some hesitation, I decided to walk across the parking lot to the diner and have something to eat while waiting for the bus to come in.

It's a big, popular diner, with many tables and a long counter. It has been there, on that same spot, for decades. The diner was crowded, since it was dinnertime. I was sitting at a small table, and near me an old man was sitting at the counter. A young and new waitress was taking the old man's order. He wanted some kind of fish. In a rather bored tone of voice, she suggested the trout almondine, and he agreed. The new waitress called out the order through the kitchen hatch. An older waitress heard the order and came over.

"Mr. Harris can't eat nuts," she said to the new waitress.

"Mr. Harris, you can't eat nuts. You can't have the trout almondine. It has almonds in it."

The old man seemed a little puzzled, but he looked back down at the menu and changed his order while the new waitress watched indifferently.

I liked the fact that the older waitress was taking care of her old steady customer. Then I had a thought that was odd, though not unpleasant: I realized I could just as easily not have witnessed this scene, if I had chosen to stay in the bus station. I could have been sitting across the parking lot in the waiting room while this scene was taking place. It would still have taken place. I had never before thought so clearly about all the scenes that took place when I wasn't there to witness them. And then, I had a stranger and less pleasant thought: not only was I not necessary to those scenes, and not necessary to those lives that continued to go on without me, but in fact, I was not necessary at all. I didn't have to exist.

I hope you understand how that is related.

When a year had passed since I had received the news, I resolved that I would at last finish my letter to you, the Foundation. It was an appropriate day on which to finish and send the letter, since it was an anniversary.

Of course, it occurred to me that another appropriate day for writing the letter might be on the final day of the grant, about a year later, and in fact another year did go by.

But that date, too, came and went without my writing or sending the letter.

Now the beginning of the award is many years in the past, and I am still teaching. It did not protect me forever from having to teach, as I was so sure it would. In fact, although I taught a little less for two years, I never stopped altogether. I did not do such good research that I would never have to teach again. I found out that if I was to continue teaching at my college, I could not stop at all.

By now, many years have also passed since I began thinking about what I wanted to write in this letter. The period of the grant is long over. You will barely remember me, even when you consult your files. I do thank you for your patience and apologize for the long delay, and please know that I remain sincerely grateful.

All my best wishes.

The Results of One
Statistical Study

People who were more conscientious
as children
lived longer.

Revise: 1

A fire does not need to be called warm or red. Remove many more adjectives.

The goose is really too silly: take the goose out. It is enough that there is a search for footprints.

The small head will be offensive: remove the small head. (But Eliot loved the small head because it was so true.) The small head is taken out, but a narrow head is put in its place.

When should the large hat appear? The woman, a traveler and teacher of the English language, was mistakenly identified by her hat and arrested for subversive activities. She could wear the large hat immediately or a little later. Should her name be Nina? The large hat is moved from the beginning to the end and then back to the beginning.

Is it fair to say he will never marry? In any case, he does become engaged to his neighbor, just in time, so it must not be said that he will never marry.

Later, Anna falls in love with a man named Hank, but it is remarked that no one would be likely to fall in love with a man named Hank. So now the man is no longer named Hank but Stefan, even though Stefan is a child living on Long Island with a sister named Anna.

Short Conversation (in Airport Departure Lounge)

"Is that a new sweater?" one woman asks another, a stranger, sitting next to her.

The other woman says it's not.

There is no further conversation.

Revise: 2

Continue with Baby but remove Priorities. Make Priorities Priority. Cut inside Moving Forward. Add to Paradox that the boredom is contained within the interest, while the interest is contained within the boredom. Take that out. Find Time. Continue with Time. Continue with Waiting. Add to Baby that its hand is grasping the foot of a strange frog. Add Priority and Nervous to Revise: 1. Continue Kingston with Family and Supermarkets. Continue with Grouch. Start Kingston with Siberian Tiger.

Left Luggage

The problem is this: she is passing through the city and needs to spend some time in the public library. But the library coat check will not accept her suitcase—she must leave it somewhere else. The answer seems clear: she will go down the street to the railway station and leave her suitcase, and then come back to the library. She walks in the wind and the rain with a small umbrella in one hand and the handle of her rolling suitcase in the other, to the railway station. She walks all over the station looking for the left-luggage office. There are restaurants and shops, a beautiful high ceiling with constellations on it, marble floors and walls, grand staircases and sloping walkways, but there is no left-luggage office. At an information window she asks about left luggage, and the angry employee silently reaches under the counter for a flyer and hands it to her. It is the flyer of a commercial left-luggage establishment that has two addresses, neither of which is in the station. She must go either several blocks uptown or several blocks down.

She walks uptown in the wind and the rain and then several blocks east, in the wrong direction, and then several blocks west, in the right direction, and finds the address, an old, narrow building between a fast-food store and a travel agent. She rides up in the elevator with a couple who are planning to get married in Brazil. They are on their way to a notary public. The woman is explaining to the man that he needs to swear before a notary that he has not been married before. Besides the notary public and the left-luggage office, this building contains a Western Union office where money can be sent or received.

The whole of the small top floor, the sixth, is the left-luggage place—one room on the street side and one in the back. The street-side room is entirely empty and flooded with sunlight. In the back room, a long folding table has been pushed across the doorway, and a man sits at the table beside a large roll of little pale blue tickets, the sort that are given out for rides at a country fair. There are some suitcases grouped against the walls in the room behind him. He smiles and speaks to her with an Eastern European accent. His smile is friendly. Some of his teeth are crooked and some are missing. She pays $10 in advance, gives the man her suitcase, and takes a pale blue ticket. Then she goes back down in the elevator and starts walking in the wind and the rain back towards the public library, thinking about her suitcase. In her haste and confusion, she has not locked it. She hopes her foreign currency won't be stolen.

She has just flown into the city from another city, in another country. They do it differently there, she thinks: in that place, there was a locker right in the middle of the station, and the locker opened onto a conveyor belt that took all the luggage to some holding area. There, she had deposited her suitcase in the locker, for a fee equivalent to $5, which seemed expensive to a man standing near her, who opened his eyes and his mouth wide and said, "*Donnerwetter!!*" When she was ready to pick up her suitcase, it was returned to her at the same place, by conveyor belt. She thinks about this as she walks. She will forget about it for a while, in the library, as she works in the quiet, chilly, thinly populated room. But as she walks, she thinks, But I am home now, and this is how we do it, in this city, in our country.

Waiting for Takeoff

We sit in the airplane so long, on the ground, waiting to take
off, that one woman declares she will now write her novel, and
another in a neighboring seat says she will be happy to edit it.
Food is being sold in the aisle, and the passengers, either hungry from waiting or worried that they will not see food again
for some time, are eagerly buying it, even food they would not
normally eat. For instance, there are candy bars long enough
to use as weapons. The steward who is selling the food says he
was once attacked by a passenger, though not with a candy bar.
Because the plane had been delayed so long, he said, the passenger threw a drink in his face, damaging one eyeball with a
piece of ice.

Industry

rant from Flaubert

How nature laughs at us—
And how impassive is the ball at which the trees dance—
and the grass, and the waves!

The bell of the steamship from Le Havre rings so furiously
I have to stop working.

What a raucous thing a *machine* is.
What a racket industry makes in the world!
How many foolish professions are born of it!
What a lot of stupidity comes from it!
Humanity is turning into an animal!

To make a *single pin* requires *five or six different specialists.*

What can you expect from the people of Manchester—
who spend their lives making *pins*?!!

The Sky Above Los Angeles

The sky is always above a tract house in Los Angeles. As the day passes, the sun comes in the large window from the east, then the south, then the west. As I look out the window at the sky, I see cumulus clouds pile up suddenly in complex, pastel-colored geometrical shapes and then immediately collapse and dissolve. After this has happened a number of times in succession, at last it seems possible for me to begin painting again.

dream

Two Characters in a Paragraph

The story is only two paragraphs long. I'm working on the end of the second paragraph, which is the end of the story. I'm intent on this work, and my back is turned. And while I'm working on the end, look what they're up to in the beginning! And they're not very far away! He seems to have drifted from where I put him and is hovering over her, only one paragraph away (in the first paragraph). True, it is a dense paragraph, and they're in the very middle of it, and it's dark in there. I knew they were both in there, but when I left it and turned to the second paragraph, there wasn't anything going on between them. Now look . . .

dream

Swimming in Egypt

We are in Egypt. We are about to go deep-sea diving. They have erected a vast tank of water on land next to the Mediterranean Sea. We strap oxygen to our backs and descend into this tank. We go all the way to the bottom. Here, there is a cluster of blue lights shining on the entrance to a tunnel. We enter the tunnel. The tunnel will lead into the Mediterranean. We swim and swim. At the far end of the tunnel, we see more lights, white ones. When we have passed through the lights, we come out of the tunnel, suddenly, into the open sea, which drops away beneath us a full kilometer or more. There are fish all around and above us, and reefs on all sides. We think we are flying, over the deep. We forget, for now, that we must be careful not to get lost, but must find our way back to the mouth of the tunnel.

dream

The Language of Things
in the House

The washing machine in spin cycle: "Pakistani, Pakistani."

The washing machine agitating (slow): "Firefighter, firefighter, firefighter, firefighter."

Plates rattling in the rack of the dishwasher: "Neglected."

The glass blender knocking on the bottom of the metal sink: "Cumberland."

Pots and dishes rattling in the sink: "Tobacco, tobacco."

The wooden spoon in the plastic bowl stirring the pancake mix: "What the hell, what the hell."

An iron burner rattling on its metal tray: "Bonanza."

•

The suction-cup pencil sharpener being peeled up from the top of the bookcase: "Rip van Winkle."

Markers rolling and bumping in a drawer that is opened and then shut: "Purple fruit."

The lid of a whipped butter tub being prised off and then put down on the counter: "Horóscopy."

A spoon stirring yeast in a bowl: "Unilateral, unilateral."

Could it be that subliminally we are hearing words and phrases all the time?

These words and phrases must be lingering in the upper part of our subconscious, readily available.

Almost always, there has to be something hollow involved: a resonating chamber.

Water going down the drain of the kitchen sink: "Late ball game."

Water running into a glass jar: "Mohammed."

The empty Parmesan cheese jar when set down on counter: "Believe me."

•

A fork clattering on the countertop: "I'll be right back."

The metal slotted spoon rattling as it is put down on the stove: "Pakistani."

A pot in the sink with water running in: "A profound respect."

A spoon stirring a mug of tea: "Iraqi, -raqi, -raqi, -raqi."

The washing machine in agitation cycle: "Pocketbook, pocketbook."

The washing machine in agitation cycle: "Corporate re-, corporate re-."

Maybe the words we hear spoken by the things in our house are words already in our brain from our reading; or from what we have been hearing on the radio or talking about to each other; or from what we often read out the car window, as for instance the sign of Cumberland Farms; or they are simply words we have always liked, such as Roanoke (as in Virginia). If these words ("Iraqi, -raqi") are in the tissue of our brain all the time, we then hear them because we hear exactly the right rhythm for the word along with more or less the right consonants and, often, something close to the right vowels. Once the rhythm and the consonants are there, our brain, having this word somewhere in it already, may be supplying the appropriate vowels.

Two hands washing in the basin: "Quote unquote."

Stove dial clicking on: "Rick."

Metal rug beater being hung up on a hook against the wooden wall of the basement stairs: "Carbohydrate."

Man's wet foot squeaking on the gas pedal: "Lisa!"

The different language sounds are created by these objects in the following way: hard consonants are created by hard objects striking hard surfaces. Vowels are created with hollow spaces, such as the inside of the butter tub whose lid and inner volume created the sounds of the word "horóscopy"—"horó" when the lid was coming off and "scopy" when the lid was put down on the counter. Some vowels, such as the e's in "neglected," spoken by the plates in the dishwater, are supplied by our brain to fill out what we hear as merely consonants: "nglctd."

Either consonants function to punctuate or to stop vowel sounds; or vowels function to fill out or to color consonants.

Wooden-handled knife hitting counter: "Background."

Plastic salad spinner being set down on counter: "Julie! Check it out!"

Drain gurgling: "Hórticult."

Orange juice container shaken once: "Genoa."

Cat jumping down onto bathroom tiles: "Va bene."

Kettle being set on clay tile: "Palermo."

Wicker laundry basket as its lid is being opened: "Vobiscum" or "Wo bist du?"

Sneeze: "At issue."

Winter jacket as it is being unzipped: "Allumettes."

Grating of wire mesh dryer filter being cleaned with fingers: "Philadelphia."

Water being sucked down drain of kitchen sink: "Dvořák."

First release of water from toilet tank as handle is depressed: "Rudolph."

I don't think I've heard or read these words recently—does this mean I always have the word "Rudolph," for instance, in my head, maybe from Rudolph Giuliani, but more probably from *"Rudolph the Red-Nosed Reindeer"*?

Zipper: "Rip."

Rattling of dishwashing utensils: "Collaboration."

Rubber flip-flop squeaking on wooden floor: "Echt."

If you hear one of these words, and pay attention, you are more likely to hear another. If you stop paying attention, you will stop hearing them.

You can hear the squawking of ducks in the scrape of a knife on a plastic cutting board. You can hear ducks, also, in the squeaking of a wet sponge rubbing a refrigerator shelf. More friction (wet sponge) will produce a squeak, whereas less friction (dry sponge) will produce a soft brushing sound. You can hear a sort of monotonous wailing music in a fan or two fans going at once if there is some slight variation in their sound.

There is no meaningful connection between the action or object that produces the sound (man's foot on gas pedal) and the significance of the word ("Lisa!").

Bird: "Dix-huit."

•

Bird: "Margueríte!"

Bird: "Hey, Frederíka!"

Soup bowl on counter: "Fabrizio!"

The Washerwomen

story from Flaubert

Yesterday I went back to a village two hours from here that I had visited eleven years ago with good old Orlowski.

Nothing had changed about the houses, or the cliff, or the boats. The women at the washing trough were kneeling in the same position, in the same numbers, and beating their dirty linen in the same blue water.

It was raining a little, like the last time.

It seems, at certain moments, as though the universe has stopped moving, as though everything has turned to stone, and only we are still alive.

How insolent nature is!

Letter to a Hotel Manager

Dear Hotel Manager,

I am writing to point out to you that the word "scrod" has been misspelled on your restaurant menu, so that it appears as "schrod," with an "sch." This word was very puzzling to me when I first read it, dining alone on the first night of my two-night stay at your hotel, in your restaurant on the ground floor off your very beautiful lobby with its carved wood panels, lofty ceiling, and rank of gold elevators. I thought this spelling must be right and I must be wrong, since here I was in New England, in Boston in fact, home of the cod and the scrod. But when I came down from my room to the lobby the following night, about to dine in your restaurant for the second time, this time with my older brother, and as I waited there in the lobby for him, which is something I generally like to do if the setting is a pleasant one and I am looking forward to a good dinner, though in fact on this occasion I was quite early and my brother was quite late, so that the wait became rather long and I began to wonder if something had happened to my brother, I was reading some literature provided to me by the friendly clerk behind the reception desk, whose manner, like that of the other staff, with the exception, perhaps, of the restaurant manager, was so natural and unaffected that my stay in your hotel was greatly enhanced by it, after I asked if he had any account of the history of your hotel, since so many interesting and famous people have stayed here or worked here or eaten or drunk here, including my own great-great-grandmother, though she was not famous, and in this literature presumably written by the hotel I read that your restaurant claimed, in fact, to have invented the word "scrod" to describe the catch of the day, in contrast to "cod," I suppose, for which this city is also famous. I also remembered, perhaps wrongly, seeing this word elsewhere spelled "shrod," unless that is a different word with a different meaning. I had thought, I suppose mistakenly, that "scrod" meant "young cod," or perhaps it was "shrod" that meant "young cod" and "scrod" that meant "catch of the day," if the word "shrod" existed at all. I don't know much about scrod, only the old joke about the two genteel ladies returning home on the train from Boston and in the course of their conversation one of them mistaking the word "scrod" for a past tense. For a moment the previous evening, as I say, I thought this spelling might even be correct, and then I was fairly certain it was not correct, but I was unsure whether it should be shrod or scrod, if the word "shrod" existed. But nowhere else have I seen it spelled "schrod," with an "sch." I did eventually, on the second evening, make a connection, perhaps a false one, between this misspelling and the accent with which your restaurant manager addressed my brother and me. This manager was present in the dining room both nights I ate there and, although courteous, seemed a bit cool in his manner, not to me in particular but to everyone, and on the second evening did not seem to want to prolong the conversation I started with him in which I suggested that the restaurant might add baked beans to the menu, since baked beans are also native to Boston and the restaurant boasts of being the inventor of Boston cream pie, the official Massachusetts state dessert, as I learned from the hotel literature, as well as the Parker House roll. He seemed almost transparently impatient to end the conversation and move on, though move on to what I did not know, since he did not appear to have more of a function than to walk rather self-importantly—by which I mean with an excessively erect posture—from one end of the long, rather dim, splendid room to the other, that is, from the wide doorway through which a handful of people now and then came in from the lobby to have dinner, to what must have been the kitchen, well hidden behind some sort of bar and two large potted palms. In any case, I noticed, as he stood conversing with us, inclined slightly towards us but at each pause turning to move away, that his accent might be identified as German, and this caused me later, when I was thinking about the misspelling of "scrod," to speculate that the very Germanic "sch" spelling was his doing. This may be quite unfair, and perhaps it was someone else, someone younger, who misspelled "scrod," and the mistake was not caught by your manager because of his Germanic predisposition towards beginning a word with "sch." Here I should add in his defense, parenthetically, that despite his cool manner he seemed quite open to my idea that baked beans might be included on the menu. He explained that at one time the restaurant had brought out little pots of baked beans with the rolls and butter at the start of the meal and that they had stopped doing this because so many other restaurants in Boston featured baked beans. I did not want him to think I liked the idea of the little pots at the start of the meal—far from it. I thought it was a terrible idea. Baked beans at the start of the meal would not be a good appetizer, being so heavy and sweet. No, no, I said, they should simply be listed somewhere on the menu. I happen to love baked beans, and I had been disappointed not to find them here in this Boston restaurant, along with the scrod, the Parker House rolls, and the Boston cream pie, all of which I ordered on the second night. My dinner companion, that is, my brother, was tolerant of this protracted and perhaps pointless conversation, either because he was happy enough to be sitting over a nice dinner and a glass of red wine after the difficult day he had had, going here and there in the city, which is not his native city, as he attempted to complete several pieces of business in connection with our mother's estate, not all of which were successful, or else because my behavior reminded him, in fact, of our mother, who was so very likely to start a conversation with a stranger, or rather, it would be more truthful to say, could hardly let a stranger come anywhere near her without striking up a conversation with him, learning something about his life and letting him know about some firmly held conviction of hers, and who passed away last fall, much to our regret. Although, naturally enough, certain of her habits bothered us while she was alive, we like to be reminded of her now, because we miss her, and we are probably both adopting some of those very habits, if we had not already adopted them long ago. I think my brother even added a suggestion of his own to the manager, after sitting listening quietly to mine, though I can't remember what he said. This was actually the second time, now at the urging of our waiter, who thought my idea was a good one, that I had called the manager over to our table. The first time I waved to him it was not to speak to him about the baked beans or the spelling of scrod but about another guest in the nearly empty dining room, a very poised little old woman, her hair in a pearl-gray bun at the nape of her neck, who sat surprisingly low down on the banquette, by the side of her much younger hired companion, so that she had to reach quite far up and out to find her food. I had noticed her during my dinner the night before, since we were near each other and there were even fewer guests, and the companion and I had at last struck up a conversation, during which I learned that the old woman lived a short walk away and had been having her dinner at the hotel every night for many years, and that in fact I was inadvertently occupying her usual spot in the dining room, under the brightest light. The companion, after consulting the old woman, had specified that she had been coming here for thirty years, which astounded me, but now, on the second night, the restaurant manager corrected this to a mere five or six years. I wanted to suggest, perhaps because I had drunk my glass of Côtes du Rhône by then and was feeling inspired, that the hotel should make a photographic portrait of her and hang it on the wall in one of the rooms, since she was now part of the history of the hotel. I still think that would be a good idea, and that you might consider it. In fact, later I got up from my chair, perhaps indiscreetly, and went over to the old woman and her companion as they were leaving and suggested the same thing, to their obvious pleasure. I did not think it would be tactful, however, to bring up the spelling of "scrod" so directly with the manager, and that is why I am instead now mentioning it in a letter to you. My stay in your grand hotel was delightful, and apart from, perhaps, the coolness of the restaurant manager, every aspect of the service and presentation was flawless except for this one spelling mistake. I do believe the purported home of the scrod should be a place where it is spelled correctly. Thank you for your attention.

Yours sincerely.

Her Birthday

105 years old:
she wouldn't be alive today
even if she hadn't died.

V

My Childhood Friend

Who is this old man walking along looking a little grim with a wool cap on his head?

But when I call out to him and he turns around, he doesn't know me at first, either—this old woman smiling foolishly at him in her winter coat.

Their Poor Dog

That irritating dog:
They didn't want it and gave it to us.
We pushed it away and smacked it on the head and tied it up.
It barked, it panted, it lunged.
We gave it back to them. They kept it for a while.

Then they sent it to an animal shelter. It was put in a concrete pen.
Visitors came and looked at it. It stood on the concrete on its four black-and-white paws.
No one wanted it.

It had no good qualities. It did not know that.
New dogs kept coming in to the shelter. After a while, they had no more space for it.

They took it into the euthanizing room to be euthanized.
It had to walk around the other dogs that were on the floor.
It leaped and pulled. It was frightened by the other dogs, and the smell.

They gave it a shot. They let it stay where it fell, and went off to get another dog.

They always took all the dead dogs out at once, at the end, to save time.

Hello Dear

Hello dear,
do you remember
how we communicated with you?

Long ago you could not see,
but I am Marina—with Russia.
Do you remember me?

I am writing this mail to you
with heavy tears in my eyes
and great sorrow in.my heart.
Come to my page.

I want you please to consider me
with so much full heartily.
Please—let us talk.

I'm waiting!

Not Interested

I'm simply not interested in reading this book. I was not interested in reading the last one I tried, either. I'm less and less interested in reading any of the books I have, though they are reasonably good, I suppose.

Just as, the other day, when I went out to the backyard, planning to gather up some sticks and branches and carry them to the pile in the far corner of the meadow, I suddenly became so deeply bored by the thought of picking up those sticks and carrying them, yet again, to that pile, and then coming back through the high meadow grass for more, that I did not even begin, and simply went inside.

Now I can do it again. It was only on that one day that I was bored. Then the feeling went away, and now I can go out again, pick up the sticks and branches, and take them to the pile. Actually, I pick up the sticks and carry them in my arms, and I drag the larger branches. I don't do both at once. I can make about three trips back and forth before I get tired and quit.

The books I'm talking about are supposed to be reasonably good, but they simply don't interest me. In fact, they may be a lot better than certain other books I have, but sometimes the books that aren't so good interest me more.

The day before that one particular day, and the day after it, I was willing to pick up sticks and take them back to the pile. Actually, for many days before, and many days after. Could I even say: all the days before that day, and all the days after? Don't ask me why I wasn't bored on other days. I've often wondered why, myself.

If I think about it, it may be that there is some satisfaction in seeing the haphazard pile of sticks and branches near the house get smaller each day, as I carry or drag them back. There is some interest, though not much, so little, in fact, that it is right on the edge of boredom, in looking at the meadow passing under my feet: the grasses, the wildflowers, and the occasional wild animal scat. Then, when I reach the brush pile in the back, there is the best moment: I weigh the bundle of sticks in my arms, or balance the branch in my two hands, and then heave them, or it, as far up to the top of the brush pile as I can. The walk back through the meadow is easy, with my arms and hands free and loose, compared to the walk out to the pile; I look around at the treetops and the sky, as well as at the house, though it never changes and is not interesting.

But on that particular day I did not even begin to feel interested in this chore, and was suddenly more deeply bored than I ever have been before, and just turned around and went back inside. Which made me wonder why I wanted to do this chore at all, on other days, and also which was real: my slight interest on other days or my profound boredom now. And it made me wonder if I really should be profoundly bored by this chore all the time and never do it again, and if there was something wrong with my mind that I was not bored by it all the time.

I'm not tired of all good books, I'm just tired of novels and stories, even good ones, or ones that are supposed to be good. These days, I prefer books that contain something real, or something the author at least believed to be real. I don't want to be bored by someone else's imagination. Most people's imagination just isn't very interesting—you can guess where the author got this idea and that idea. You can predict what will come next before you finish reading one sentence. It all seems so arbitrary.

But it's true that I'm also bored, sometimes, by my own

dreams, and by the act of dreaming: here I go again, this scene does not make sense, I must be falling asleep, this is a dream, I'm about to start dreaming again. And I am sometimes bored even by the act of thinking: Here's another thought, I'm about to find it interesting or not interesting—not this again! In fact, I am sometimes bored by my friendships: Oh, we will spend the evening together, we will talk, then I will go home—this again!

Actually, I don't mean I'm bored by old novels and books of stories if they're good. Just new ones—good or bad. I feel like saying: Please spare me your imagination, I'm so tired of your vivid imagination, let someone else enjoy it. That's how I'm feeling these days, anyway, maybe it will pass.

Old Woman, Old Fish

The fish that has been sitting in my stomach all afternoon was so old by the time I cooked and ate it, no wonder I am uncomfortable—an old woman digesting an old fish.

Staying at the Pharmacist's

story from Flaubert

Where am I staying? In the home of a pharmacist! Yes, but whose student is he? *Dupré's!* Isn't that fantastic?

Like Dupré, he makes a lot of seltzer water.

"I'm the only one in Trouville who makes seltzer water," he says.

And it's true that often, as early as eight o'clock in the morning, I am woken by the noise of corks flying away: *pif, paf,* and *cccrrrout!*

The kitchen is also the laboratory. Among the saucepans, there rises, in an arc, from a monstrous still, a

fearful tube of steaming copper

and often they can't put the pot on the fire because of the pharmaceutical preparations.

To go to the shithouse in the courtyard, you have to step over baskets filled with bottles. They have a pump out there that spits water and sprays your legs. The two boys rinse jars. A parrot squawks over and over all day long: "Have you had lunch, Jako?" or "Coco, my little Coco!" And a kid of about ten, the son of the house, the great hope of the pharmacy, practices feats of strength by lifting weights with his teeth.

A piece of foresight which I find touching is that there's always paper in the WC—*gummed paper* or, rather, *waxed paper*. It's the wrapping from packages—they don't know what else to do with it.

The pharmacist's latrine is so small and dark that you have to leave the door open when you crap, and you can hardly move your elbows to wipe your ass.

The family dining room is right there, close by.

You hear the sound of the turds falling into the *can*, mingled with the sound of pieces of meat being turned over on the plates. Belches alternating with farts, etc.—charming.

And that eternal parrot! Right now it's whistling: "I've got good tobacco, yes I do!"

The Song

Something has happened, in a house, and then something else has happened, but no one is bothered. The light, pleasant voice of a man begins to sing in an upstairs hallway, aimlessly, steadily. We hardly notice. Then, from the bottom of the stair-well, abruptly, comes the savage shout of another man: "Who sing!?!" The singing voice falls silent.

dream

Two Former Students

One former student told the other former student to go away, out there, in the snow, at night.

Go away, he said to the other. If she sees us both, she will label us both former students, forgetting that I am I and you are you.

He was the older former student. He had fought in a war. He had not reenlisted because he wanted to do something else with his life. He was deaf in one ear.

The other former student was young, but he had been to Europe.

It was true that as she looked out the window at them walking back and forth under the streetlight, they were, in her mind, two former students, more so than if each of them had been alone, fully himself, though also, unavoidably, a former student.

dream

A Small Story About a Small Box of Chocolates

A very kind man had made a little gift to her, on her visit to Vienna that fall, of a box of chocolates. The box was so small it could sit in the palm of her hand, and yet, as though by a miracle, it contained 32 tiny, perfect chocolates, all different, in two layers of 16 each.

She had carried it home from Vienna without eating any, as she always carried home food that she acquired on a trip. She wanted to show it to her husband, and she intended to share it with him. But after she opened the box and they both admired the chocolates, she shut the box again without taking a chocolate and without offering him one, and put the box away in her private workplace. There she kept it and looked at it from time to time.

She thought of sharing it with her students the next time she went to class, but she did not take it.

She did not open the box and her husband did not ask about the chocolates either. She could not believe he had forgotten them, since she herself thought of them and looked at the box so often. But after a couple of weeks, she had to believe he had forgotten about them.

She thought of having one chocolate each day, but she did not want to begin eating the chocolates without some special occasion.

She thought of sharing the box with 31 friends, but she could not decide when to begin that.

Finally, when the end of the semester and the last night of her class came, she decided to take the chocolates with her and share them. She was afraid she had waited too long, since four weeks had passed since the kind man had given her the chocolates in Vienna, and the chocolates might be stale, but she put rubber bands around the box and took it anyway.

She told her students how it amazed her to think that a box of chocolates so small could be shared with 31 friends. She thought they would laugh, but they did not. Perhaps they were not sure if it would be polite to laugh, or perhaps they did not think that what she had said was funny. She could not always predict their reactions. She herself thought it was funny, or at least interesting.

She took the lid off the box and handed it to the nearest student. She invited them all to admire the chocolates.

"Can we also eat one?" asked the student who was holding the box, "or should we just look at them?" He was perhaps joking, but perhaps she had not been clear that she was sharing the chocolates with them.

"Of course you should eat them," she said.

"May I see the lid of the box?" asked another student.

The lid was almost as beautiful as the chocolates. It was green and closely decorated with little medieval figures and buildings in orange, yellow, black, white, and gold. On little white banners, black letters in German Gothic script spelled out what seemed to be proverbs—short sayings that rhymed. She could understand only a few words of each proverb. One recommended acting like a sundial.

The hungry students each took one tiny chocolate—or perhaps, since she was not watching them closely, some took none and some took more than one. She had planned to share the chocolates with 31 different friends, but now she felt sorry for the tired, hungry students and sent the box around the room again. One student, a young man from Canada, took responsibility for gathering up the tiny empty paper holders from inside the box and carrying them to the wastebasket by the classroom door.

After the class, she put the rubber bands around the box again and carried it back home.

She herself had not yet eaten a chocolate, and she was a little worried that she had waited too long. How long could one keep chocolates sitting in a box? She had been afraid the chocolates would taste stale to the students. But only one student was an expert in chocolates, she was sure. That student would not say anything, out of politeness, or perhaps had not even taken a chocolate, knowing how long ago she had been in Vienna.

Then, two days later, she could not find the box in her bag or her briefcase and was afraid she had lost it. She even thought for a moment that perhaps a student had stolen it.

Then she looked more carefully and found it. She opened the box and counted: 7 chocolates out of 32 remained in the box—25 had been eaten. Yet there were only 11 students in the class.

She put it once again in her workplace, on the old Mexican bench that she liked so much.

She wondered whether it was right to eat a chocolate by herself, and, if it was right, then whether one had to be in a certain mood or frame of mind to eat a chocolate by oneself. It did not seem right to eat a chocolate out of anger, or resentment, or greed, but only out of a lust for pleasure, or in a mood of happiness or celebration. But if one did eat a chocolate by oneself out of greed, was it less wrong if the chocolate was very small?

She knew that she did not want to share the remaining chocolates.

When at last she ate a chocolate, by herself, it was very good, rich and bitter, sweet and strange at the same time. The taste of it remained in her mouth minute after minute, so that she wanted to eat another one, to begin the pleasure all over again. She had planned to eat one each day until they were gone. But now she ate another right away. She wanted to eat a third, but did not. The next day, she ate two, one after the other, out of a lust for pleasure, in defiance of what she thought was right. And the next day, she ate one more out of a vague, indefinite hunger, not necessarily for food.

She found the chocolates so good that she decided she had not waited too long, after all. Unless she was not qualified to judge, and there was a difference, imperceptible to her but perceptible to an expert, such as the one student she believed was an expert, between the taste of a chocolate eaten right away and one eaten after four weeks.

Then she asked her student, the expert in good chocolates, where in the city she could buy the best chocolates. Her student gave her the name of the best store for chocolates, and she went to that store hoping to find tiny chocolates like those given to her by the kind man in Vienna. But the store offered only larger chocolates, chocolates of a more typical size, good in their own way but not what she wanted.

She did not like to eat larger chocolates, she decided. Now that she had, for the first time, experienced the tiniest of chocolates, that was what she preferred.

She had, some months before, been offered a chocolate in Connecticut, in the home of a rather severe Belgian woman whom she had known for many years. It had been a good chocolate, as far as she could tell, but she had found it a little too large, too large to eat quickly, in any case. She had taken many small bites of it, and enjoyed those bites, but had not wanted another chocolate when urged. The other people present had found that strange, and the Belgian woman had laughed at her.

The Woman Next to Me
on the Airplane

The woman next to me has many fast and easy crossword puzzles to do during the flight, from a book called *Fast and Easy Crosswords.* I have only slow and difficult crosswords, or impossible crosswords. She finishes each puzzle and turns the page, as we fly at top speed through the air. I stare at one page and don't finish any.

Writing

Life is too serious for me to go on writing. Life used to be easier, and often pleasant, and then writing was pleasant, though it also seemed serious. Now life is not easy, it has gotten very serious, and by comparison, writing seems a little silly. Writing is often not about real things, and then, when it is about real things, it is often at the same time taking the place of some real things. Writing is too often about people who can't manage. Now I have become one of those people. I am one of those people. What I should do, instead of writing about people who can't manage, is just quit writing and learn to manage. And pay more attention to life itself. The only way I will get smarter is by not writing anymore. There are other things I should be doing instead.

Wrong Thank-You in Theater

At the back of the auditorium, as the theater fills for the event, I stand up from my seat to let a woman get past me to her seat in the row.

"Thanks," she says.

"Mmm-hmm!" I say in acknowledgment.

But I have misunderstood. She was not thanking me, she was thanking the usher, who is standing a few feet behind me.

"No, I meant *her*," she says, without looking at me.

She just wanted to make that clear.

The Rooster

Today I paid a condolence call on Safwan, the owner of the Farm and Country Deli. His rooster was killed last week on the road. I had first stopped at the house across from the deli, where there are many chickens and three roosters—but it was not one of those that had been killed. I talked to Safwan for a little while. He said he would not be getting another rooster— the road was too dangerous. His rooster had often wandered into the road pecking at crumbs, Safwan said, instead of staying in the backyard, because of the dog in the yard next door, which frightened him.

After I had paid my condolence call, I picked up two of the rooster's oily green feathers from the side of the road for a keepsake, and returned home. I sent my friend Rachel a message telling her that I was sad about Safwan's rooster, whose regular cry all day long had made me happy. Each time I heard it, I felt I was really living out in the country—at least farther out in the country than I had been in my last place.

Rachel, who always has many lines of poetry in her head, sent me in return some lines from a poem by Elizabeth Bishop: "Oh, why should a *hen*/have been run over/on West 4th Street . . . ?" I liked the lines, though I had trouble imagining a hen alive on West 4th Street, let alone a hen that had been run over. I then found another line by Elizabeth Bishop about a hen, in a poem about a hermit and some train tracks: "The pet hen went chook-chook." To me, "chook-chook" sounded more like a train than the hen.

Later I met some neighbors of mine who had witnessed the accident. They said they had been driving south in their van towards the deli when they saw the rooster in the road in front of them. At the same time, there was a tractor-trailer coming from the opposite direction, north towards the deli. The rooster had hastened to get out of the way of the van, and in his haste had run straight into the path of the tractor-trailer. The neighbors smiled as they told the story. I suppose they were amused by the violence of the impact and the sight of the bird exploding up into the air off the front of the truck, feathers everywhere.

A few days later I realized that there might have been another reason why the rooster had wandered over to the far side of the road. He was the only bird that Safwan owned. He might have gone across the road to visit the neighbors' chicken coop with its little crowd of hens and roosters. He was probably interested in them and liked to watch them through their fence, maybe even try to challenge the other roosters. I realized this when I was studying a book about raising poultry: hens and roosters are sociable creatures and prefer to be part of a flock, it said. When you are ready to buy your chicks, be sure to buy at least five.

Sitting with My Little Friend

Sitting with my little friend in the sunshine on the front
step:
　　I am reading a book by Blanchot
　　and she is licking her leg.

The Old Soldier

story from Flaubert

I saw something the other day that moved me, though I had nothing to do with it. We were three miles from here, at the ruins of the Château de Lassay (built in six weeks for Madame Du Barry, who had the idea of coming to take sea baths in the area). There's nothing left but a staircase, a large Louis XV staircase, a few windows without panes, a wall, and wind . . . wind! It's on a plateau within sight of the sea. Next to it is a peasant hut. We went in to get a drink of milk for Liline, who was thirsty. The little garden had lovely hollyhocks as high as the eaves, a few rows of beans, a cauldron full of dirty water. Nearby a pig was grunting, and farther off, beyond the enclosure, unfenced foals grazed and whinnied, their full, flowing manes moving in the wind from the sea.

Inside the hut, on the wall, was a picture of the Emperor and another of Badinguet! I was probably about to make some joke, when I saw, sitting in a corner by the fireplace, half paralyzed, a thin old man with a two-week-old beard. Above his armchair, hanging on the wall, were two gold epaulettes! The poor old man was so infirm that he had trouble holding his spoon. No one was paying any attention to him. He sat there ruminating, groaning, eating from a platter of beans. The sun shone in the window onto the iron bands around the buckets, making him squint. The cat lapped milk from a pan on the floor. And that was all. In the distance, the vague sound of the sea.

I thought about how, in this perpetual half-sleep of old age (which precedes the other sleep, and is a sort of transition from life to nothingness), the fellow no doubt was seeing once again the snows of Russia or the sands of Egypt. What visions were floating before those cloudy eyes? And what clothes he wore! What a jacket—patched and clean! The woman who served us (his daughter, I imagine) was a fifty-year-old gossip in a short skirt, with calves like the balusters in the Place Louis XV and a cotton cap on her head. She came and went in her blue stockings and coarse skirt, and splendid Badinguet was there in the midst of it all, mounted on a yellow horse, three-cornered hat in hand, saluting a cohort of war wounded, their wooden legs all precisely aligned.

The last time I visited the Château de Lassay was with Alfred. I can still remember the conversation we had, the verses we recited, the plans we made . . .

Two Sligo Lads

Two Sligo lads are on their way to work at an immense factory that looms up ahead of them on the horizon. Abruptly, then, they are whirled up into a fairground ride consisting of spinning cars moving in elliptical arcs, so far above me that they are mere specks in the sky. As they revolve, crossing over and over, they cry out to me "Hello, hello," again and again, at irregular intervals. Then the ride is gone, but they are still there, circling. They might now be seagulls.

dream

The Woman in Red

Standing near me is a tall woman in a dark red dress. She has a dazed, rather blank expression on her face. She might be drugged, or this is simply her habitual expression. I am a little afraid of her. A red snake in front of me rears up and threatens me, at the same time changing form once or twice, acquiring tentacles like a squid, etc. Behind it is a large puddle of water in the middle of a broad path. To protect me from the snake, the woman in the red dress lays three broad-brimmed red hats down on the surface of the puddle of water.

dream

If at the Wedding (at the Zoo)

If we hadn't stopped on our way to the ceremony to look at the pen of black pigs, we wouldn't have seen the very large pig lunge at the smaller one, to force him away from the feeding trough.

If we hadn't come early and seated ourselves on a bench in the sunlight under the pavilion roof to await the start of the ceremony, we wouldn't have seen the runaway pony trot past trailing its rope.

If we hadn't heard the sudden murmur of our neighbors on the benches in the cold sunlight under the pavilion before the start of the ceremony, we wouldn't have looked up to see the bride coming in her bright green dress from a distance walking briskly with long strides hand in hand with her mother.

If we hadn't craned our necks to look around the people standing in front of us prepared to officiate and take part in the ceremony, we wouldn't have seen how the bride came, her head bowed, her mother's head bowed, her mother talking seriously to her, the two of them never looking up, as though there were no one else present, towards the pavilion, the guests, the poised cameras, the ceremony, and her future husband, who stood waiting for her.

If we hadn't looked away from the ceremony in which the couple getting married stood before their officiating Buddhist friend while their other assembled friends and family chanted Indian and other chants, we wouldn't have seen the Hasidic and Asian families walk past the pavilion gazing curiously at us on their way to and from the Corn Maze.

If we hadn't walked across the room in which the reception was beginning, past the two accordionists, man and woman, to look out the back windows at the wedding party being photographed in the cold October sunlight late in the day to the sound of klezmer music, we wouldn't have seen the two families of pheasants run along the crest of the pumpkin field towards the shelter of the woods.

If we hadn't walked across the reception room to stand next to strangers at the back windows, we wouldn't have seen the wedding party being photographed with their faces towards the setting sun, holding one another in the cold, laughing and stumbling as they changed positions and poses between shots, with accordion music behind us in our background so that the scene we were watching was suddenly like the end of a happy Italian movie.

If we hadn't returned to look out the back windows later during the reception, after the speeches in the far corner of the room and after the dinner sitting close to people we knew but across from strangers, we wouldn't have seen the brown cow raise her nose and toss her head, standing under a tree, and chew her cud looking up at the sky.

If we hadn't left the reception hall for a moment after dark, before coming back in to the light and music and dancing, we wouldn't have seen the black round shapes in the branches of the trees, which were the chickens roosting.

The Gold Digger of Goldfields

It was called Goldfields, it was a ghost town—boarded-up saloons, population 100. The wells were poisoned with arsenic, still are. We found that out later. Jim's stepmother had cancer, maybe from the arsenic in the wells. Jim's father was selling off his coin collection a little at a time to pay for her treatment. She got worse and he flew her back to the cancer hospital, but it was too late. She died.

Two weeks later, they sent Jim a message about his father—there's a medical emergency, come out right away. We drove thirty-six hours straight. But he was dead, too, by the time we got there.

We didn't know about whatever it's called—compassionate airfare. We'd already driven through five states by the time someone told us about that. Jim said, We've already driven this far—we're driving.

Jim got sleepy after twenty-four hours and let me drive. But he can't sleep in the car, so after three hours he took over again. Alyce kept texting us to come home. I told her to do her homework and stop worrying. She had no idea how far away we were.

Where *are* you? she kept saying. She thought we were in New Jersey. Where? *Nevada?* she kept asking.

Go get a map, I said.

We didn't know what we'd find when we got there.

Jim's sister Lisa, the one I call the gold digger, had looked all over for what was left of the coins, she wanted more money for caring for him. She said she had no money to bury him. She said they had to take their tax money to have him cremated.

When we got there, we kept finding coins all over the house. Piles of coins. Lisa, the gold digger, didn't find them. She didn't know where to look. She took all the guns out, though, before we got there.

Jim's other sister, the executor, told us (from New Jersey) to get all his papers together. Jim couldn't do it, he wasn't up to it. He would go into his father's bedroom and just sit there. That's all he could do. I did it. I knew him, but I wasn't that close to him. I went through all the papers, sorted them, put them in files by year.

I said to Lisa, You should see a psychiatrist—after being so close to him, all you want is his coin collection? Why didn't you take it before he died?

She thought she should have gotten more because she took care of him. That's not what was in the will.

We drove thirty-six hours straight going back, too. Hitting the deer on the way home was the last straw for Jim. He used some language about that.

The other sister, the executor, wanted us to come to New Jersey. Jim kept saying no, we want to get home. She kept asking us to come. Finally he said we would. It was when we were in Pennsylvania forking off towards New Jersey that we hit the deer. It was a rental car, so we had to wait there for the police so we could file a report. One headlight was broken. It cost $1,000 to repair. The insurance didn't pay for it because there was a $1,000 deductible.

All Jim wanted was something like a belt buckle to remember him by. A silver belt buckle. I said to his sister the gold digger, You should see a psychiatrist.

Jim's father had a water cooler in his house. I always wondered why he had a water cooler. Now I know.

The Old Vacuum Cleaner Keeps
Dying on Her

The old vacuum cleaner keeps dying on her
over and over
until at last the cleaning woman
scares it by yelling:
"Motherfucker!"

Flaubert and Point of View

At the Blessing of the Hounds, on the opening day of fox-hunting season, a Saturday (large horses sleekly groomed, men and women in red riding costumes seated on them or holding them by the bridle, a little girl less interested in the horses than in her friend across the road, as small as she is, almost small enough to walk right under the bellies of these tall horses, the duck or goose that can be heard in the occasional silence squawking in the brook down below the country store, the car that now and then approaches this congested small country square and then turns around as best it can, the two pug dogs held on a leash by an elderly woman who says that she has brought them to see the Blessing of the Hounds, the onlookers holding their coffee cups steaming in the cool early-morning air, the pack of hunting dogs milling about loose in the road, tightly controlled by the handler with her long whip, the speech of the Master of the Hounds and the silences as he pauses with bowed head between remarks, when the duck or goose can be heard squawking), I am reminded, at last, of Flaubert's lesson concerning the singular point of view, not by the little girl interested mainly in her friend, the other little girl, or by the duck or goose interested only in whatever it is that is making it squawk down below in the brook, but by the two pug dogs, as they strain at their leashes to reach one particular spot on the ground, intent not on the horses, the riders, the speech of the Master of the Hounds, the hunting dogs, or the squawking duck or goose, but only on the yellowish-white dollops of foam that have dropped from the mouth of a high-spirited horse nearby onto the dark pavement and that are so strange to them and so fragrant.

Family Shopping

The plump, pretty younger sister is running out of the store. The thin, older sister is running after her. The pretty younger sister is carrying a bag of cheese twists. She had left the thin older sister behind in the store to pay for them.

"*Give* that to me!" says the older sister. "I'll wring your *neck*!"

Local Obits

Helen loved long walks, gardening, and her grandchildren.

Richard founded his own business.

Anna later helped on the family farm.

Robert enjoyed his home.

Alfred enjoyed his best friends, which were his two cats.

Henry enjoyed woodworking.

Ed loved life and lived it to the fullest.

John enjoyed fishing and woodworking.

•

"Tootles" enjoyed puzzles of all kinds, painting items her husband built, and keeping in touch with family and friends via the computer.

Tammy enjoyed reading and bowling. She bowled in the Mixed League at the Barbecue Recreation Lanes.

Margaret enjoyed watching NASCAR, doing crossword puzzles, and spending time with her grandchildren.

Eva was an avid gardener, bird watcher, and also enjoyed reading and writing poetry. She loved entertaining.

Madeleine traveled extensively. She enjoyed painting, ceramics, bridge, golf, any card game, word search puzzles, gardening, coin and stamp collecting, and flower arranging. She loved visiting with friends both at camp and at the family home on Main Street.

Albert was an animal lover.

Jean, a special-ed aide, liked to crochet and knit.

Harold enjoyed hunting, fishing, camping, and time spent with family.

•

Charlotte was an avid quilter, and also loved picking blueberries on her farm in Taborton.

Alvin was a skilled craftsman and gardener. He was also an avid sportsman, enjoying trout fishing, ice fishing, grouse and deer hunting. He was a member of the Ruffed Grouse Society.

Richard enjoyed his favorite hobbies of fishing and boating, and was a thirty-year member of the Hook Boat Club.

Sven, 80, a builder, was a member of the Free and Accepted Masons, the Nordic Glee Club, and the American Union of Swedish Singers. He liked to travel, hunt, golf, and throw parties. He was most often found in his workshop building something.

Spencer poured his remaining years into milking cows and tilling the land. He always liked the smell of fresh-cut hay on a hot summer day. He loved the animals and seemed like he could live in the barn. He always spoke of the old days when the neighborhood was all farmers and how they would always lend a helping hand. Sons and nephews who worked with him found it hard to keep pace even though they were twenty to thirty years younger. He lived a full life, continuing to do tractor work on the farm even after it was sold.

He also enjoyed watching football in the fall, and always said Joe Montana was the best QB to play the game.

In later years, he liked to visit Stewart's regularly with his brother Harold and watch the people. He had the gift of gab; with anyone who knew him or even didn't know him, he would strike up an hour-long conversation.

Helena, 70, liked long walks.

Mrs. Brown was a registered nurse for thirty-two years. She was very fond of the nursing field.

Roxanna was an avid golfer and bowler, and loved crocheting and oil and watercolor painting.

Frederick was the owner of Half Moon Saloon for ten years and was a member of the Elks Lodge, where he served as past exalted ruler for a year.

Benjamin, 91, was a WWII vet and a brick mason.

Jessie, 93, worked at area factories in her younger years. She enjoyed gardening and bowling.

Anne, 51, enjoyed fishing and gardening.

Eleanor worked for Dandy Laundry and Cleaners for twenty-seven years and for local families in a domestic capacity.

Dick was meticulous in the care he gave to his home, yard, and automobiles.

Earlier in her career, Elizabeth, known as "Betty," spent her free time with soldiers returning from the war—dancing, playing Ping-Pong, and talking. She sang in the church choir and served briefly as church treasurer.

Laura enjoyed playing cards, doing puzzles, and traveling.

Jeffrey enjoyed golfing and working on the family farm.

Stella was known for her love of cats.

Marion, 100, was a homemaker her entire life. She enjoyed playing cards at the Senior Center and going on her many trips to Colorado. She always looked for the good in people.

Nellie, 79, was employed at the former Snow White Laundry. She enjoyed playing bingo, doing jigsaw puzzles, and spending time with family. She is predeceased by a brother, eight sisters, and one boy she helped to raise.

John, 73, died suddenly after being stricken while driving in Grafton. He was an avid hunter who enjoyed farming.

Clyde, 90, served in the Navy during WWII and was a meat cutter by trade. He was a member of the American Legion, the Stephentown Fire Company, the Tamarac Twirlers, the Quadrille Square Dance Club, and the Albany Camera Club.

With regrets, Mary Ellen leaves behind her son James, her sister Theresa, her companion Rich, and her brother Harold. Anyone who knew her, knew her love for Tigger.

Elva, 81, attended the two-room schoolhouse in North Petersburgh.

Evelyn, 87, worked at Montgomery Ward in Menands and was also a waitress at the Crooked Lake Hotel. She enjoyed the horses at Saratoga and loved to sing and dance. Throughout the early part of her life, she often partnered with Billy Nassau at the Cat in the Fiddle Restaurant.

Linda Ann is also survived by her cat, Sable, and her dog, Socks. She will be remembered for her book collection, especially those written by her favorite author, Nora Roberts, and for her gifts to family and friends of pillowcases she embroidered. She will also be remembered for her extensive collection of elephant figurines.

Bernie, 86, was a member of the Derby Club, the Hoosick Falls Fire Department, the Hoosick Falls Rescue Squad, the Kiwanis, the Veterans of Foreign Wars, the Knights of Columbus, the Pioneer Fish and Game Club, and the Hoot 'n Holler Club. He was interested in fishing, hunting, gardening, and beekeeping.

•

Robert, 83, was predeceased by his wife, Anne, known as "Nancy." He served in the U.S. Navy as a petty officer, third class, and was honored with a Victory Medal.

Alvin, 88, liked to fish, paint, garden, cook, and watch the Yankees.

Paul, 78, worked on county highways, was a member of the famed Keyser's Softball Team, and loved to bowl and jitterbug with his sister Babe.

Virginia, 99, was a grandmother and church member.

Robert, 81, was an evening manager at the Grand Union.

Isabel, 95, was a mother and grandmother.

Donald was an inspiration to all.

Jerold, 72, cook and counselor, worked as a mover for many years and loved attending fairs, wandering country roads, "anything Vermont," and playing Father Christmas.

Francis, 79, Korean War vet and soils expert, retired as drill supervisor. He was an avid sportsman and trivia whiz. He was a member of the American Legion, the Kinderhook Elks Lodge, the Veterans of Foreign Wars, the Tin Can Sailors-National Association of Destroyer Vets, the Men's Club of Five Towns, the Saints Social Club, and the ROMEOs. His quick wit, easy smile, and legendary handlebar mustache will be sorely missed.

Margaret, 88, church member and Yankees fan, loved traveling with her late husband to engine and tractor shows all over the nation.

Betty, 81, secretary, enjoyed spending time with her grand-children.

William, 81, had a passion for history and genealogy.

Gordon, 68, an avid hunter, died peacefully at the Firemen's Home on Monday.

Ronald, 72, former fire chief and retired truck driver, was an avid duck hunter.

Ellen, 87, volunteered at the Amtrak Station Snack Bar.

Joseph, 76, peacefully fell asleep in death in the cool early morning of August 26. He was best known in the community as a master plumber, and until his death was an active member of the Federation of Polish Sportsmen. He loved his wife and family. He loved his thirty-five race horses, but loved one especially, his stallion Bright Cat, who died earlier this year.

Ida, 95, put friends and family first.

John, 74, a veteran, worked for the Thruway Authority.

Ruth, 85, was a passionate animal lover and wildlife observer.

Anne, 62, found joy in felines, especially her friends Daisy, Rigel, Grace, Luci, Celeste, and Smokey.

Ernest, 85, was a merchant marine during WWII, often sailing in enemy waters. He later worked as a welder and repairman, and enjoyed woodworking after his retirement.

Edwin, 94, left one daughter.

Diane, 60, was a beauty school grad and upholsterer.

James, 87, worked for many years as a laurel picker for Engwer Florist Supply of Troy. He loved gardening, canning, wine-making, and putting down a crock of green tomatoes or sauerkraut.

Dolores, 83, a seamstress, had a sense of humor. In her earlier days, she worked at the Kadin Brothers Pocketbook Factory.

Letter to the President of the American Biographical Institute, Inc.

Dear President,

I was pleased to receive your letter informing me that I had been nominated by the Governing Board of Editors as WOMAN OF THE YEAR—2006. But at the same time I was puzzled. You say that this award is given to women who have set a "noble" example for their peers, and that your desire is, as you put it, to "uplift" their accomplishments. You then say that in researching my qualifications, you were assisted by a Board of Advisors consisting of 10,000 "influential" people living in seventy-five countries. Yet even after this extensive research, you have made a basic factual mistake and addressed your letter, not to Lydia Davis, which is my name, but to Lydia Danj.

Of course, it may be that you do not have my name wrong but that you are awarding your honor to an actual Lydia Danj. But either mistake would suggest a lack of care on your part. Should I take this to mean that there was no great care taken over the research upon which the award is based, despite the involvement of 10,000 people? This would suggest that I should not place great importance on the honor itself. Furthermore, you invite me to send for tangible proof of this nomination in the form of what you call a "decree," presented by the American Biographical Institute Board of International Research, measuring 11 × 14 inches, limited and signed. For a plain decree you ask me to pay $195, while a laminated decree will cost me $295.

Again, I am puzzled. I have received awards before, but I was not asked to pay anything for them. The fact that you have mistaken my name and that you are also asking me to pay for my award suggests to me that you are not truly honoring me but rather want me to believe I am being honored so that I will send you either $195 or $295. But now I am further puzzled.

I would assume that any woman who is truly accomplished in the world, whose accomplishments "to date," as you say, are outstanding and deserve what you call top honors, would be intelligent enough not to be misled by this letter from you. And yet your list must consist of women who have accomplished something, because a woman who had accomplished nothing at all would surely not believe that her accomplishments deserved a "Woman of the Year" award.

Could it be, then, that what your research produces is a list of women who have accomplished enough so that they may believe they do indeed deserve a "Woman of the Year" award and yet are not intelligent or worldly enough to see that for you this is a business and there is no real honor involved? Or are they women who have accomplished something they believe is deserving of honor and are intelligent enough to know, deep down, that you are in this only for profit, yet, at the same time, are willing to part with $195 or $295 to receive this decree, either plain or laminated, perhaps not admitting to themselves that it means nothing?

If your research has identified me as a member of one of these two groups of women—either easily deceived concerning communications from organizations like yours or willing to deceive themselves, which I suppose is worse—then I am sorry and I must wonder what it suggests about me. But on the other hand, since I feel I really do not belong to either of these two groups, perhaps this is simply more evidence that your research has not been good and you were mistaken to include me, whether as Lydia Davis or as Lydia Danj, on your list. I look forward to hearing your thoughts on this.

Yours sincerely.

Nancy Brown Will Be in Town

Nancy Brown will be in town. She will be in town to sell her things. Nancy Brown is moving far away. She would like to sell her queen mattress.

Do we want her queen mattress? Do we want her ottoman? Do we want her bath items?

It is time to say goodbye to Nancy Brown.

We have enjoyed her friendship. We have enjoyed her tennis lessons.

Ph.D.

All these years I thought I had a Ph.D.
But I do not have a Ph.D.

Notes and Acknowledgments

The stories in this collection first appeared in the following publications, sometimes in slightly different form:

32 Poems: "Men"
Bodega: "Idea for a Sign"
Bomb: "A Woman, Thirty"
Cambridge Literary Review: "Revise: 1," "Revise: 2"
Conjunctions: "Reversible Story"
dOCUMENTA (13) Notebooks series: "Two Former Students"
Electric Literature: "The Cows"
Fence: "At the Bank," "At the Bank: 2," "The Churchyard," "The Gold Digger of Goldfields," "In the Train Station," "The Moon"
Five Dials (U.K.): "Notes During Long Phone Conversation with Mother," "On the Train," "A Story of Stolen Salamis," "A Story Told to Me by a Friend," "Nancy Brown Will Be in Town"
Five Points: "A Note from the Paperboy," "Her Birthday"
Gerry Mulligan: "Left Luggage"
gesture zine: "The Problem of the Vacuum Cleaner," "The Old Vacuum Cleaner Keeps Dying on Her"
Granta: "The Dreadful Mucamas"
Harlequin: "Wrong Thank-You in Theater"
Harper's: "How I Read as Quickly as Possible Through My Back Issues of the *TLS*," "The Two Davises and the Rug"
Hodos: "Old Woman, Old Fish"

Little Star: "Handel," "Housekeeping Observation," "Judgment," "Sitting with My Little Friend," "The Sky Above Los Angeles"

Mississippi Review: "A Small Story About a Small Box of Chocolates," "Her Geography: Alabama," "Her Geography: Illinois," "I'm Pretty Comfortable, But I Could Be a Little More Comfortable," "The Washerwomen"

MLS: "Contingency (vs. Necessity) 2: On Vacation," "Hello Dear," "I Ask Mary About Her Friend, the Depressive, and His Vacation," "Letter to the President of the American Biographical Institute, Inc.," "Molly, Female Cat: History/Findings"

New American Writing: "The Old Soldier," "Staying at the Pharmacist's," "Flaubert and Point of View"

NOON: "Bloomington," "The Cornmeal," "Dinner," "The Dog Hair," "How I Know What I Like (Six Versions)," "The Language of the Telephone Company," "Learning Medieval History," "Master," "My Footsteps," "Not Interested," "The Party," "Ph.D.," "The Song," "Their Poor Dog," "Writing"

Pear Noir!: "The Bad Novel," "Waiting for Takeoff," "The Woman Next to Me on the Airplane"

PEN America: "The Landing"

Plume: "Brief Incident in Short *a*, Long *a*, and Schwa," "Contingency (vs. Necessity)," "My Friend's Creation," "Ödön von Horváth Out Walking"

Salt Hill: "Circular Story," "Grade Two Assignment," "Short Conversation (in Airport Departure Lounge)"

Satori: "The Force of the Subliminal"

Sous Rature: "The Husband-Seekers," "The Low Sun," "Two Sligo Lads"

Story Quarterly: "The Woman in Red"

The Coffin Factory: "Negative Emotions," "The Rooster"

The Iowa Review: "The Child," "The Dog," "The Grandmother"

The Literary Review: "Letter to a Frozen Peas Manufacturer," "Letter to a Hotel Manager," "Letter to a Peppermint Candy Company"

The Los Angeles Review: "The Sentence and the Young Man"

The New York Times: "The Seals" (original title "Everyone Was Invited")

The Paris Review: "The Cook's Lesson," "After You Left," "The Visit to the Dentist," "Pouchet's Wife," "The Funeral," "The Coachman and the Worm," "The Execution," "The Chairs," "The Exhibition," "My School Friend," "Local Obits," "The Language of Things in the House," "If at the Wedding (at the Zoo)," "The Results of One Statistical Study," "My Childhood Friend"

The Threepenny Review: "The Letter to the Foundation"

The World: "My Sister and the Queen of England"

Tim: "Two Characters in a Paragraph," "Two Undertakers"

Tin House: "Eating Fish Alone," "In the Gallery," "The Piano," "The Piano Lesson," "The Schoolchildren in the Large Building," "Swimming in Egypt"

Tolling Elves: "Family Shopping"

Upstreet: "An Awkward Situation"

Wave Composition: "Industry"

Western Humanities Review: "Awake in the Night," "The Bodyguard," "*Can't* and *Won't*," "The Last of the Mohicans"

"If at the Wedding (at the Zoo)" is dedicated to Joanna Sondheim and Eugene Lim.

"A Small Story About a Small Box of Chocolates" is dedicated to Rainer Goetz.

"The Landing" also appeared in *The Daily Telegraph* (U.K.).

"The Seals" also appeared, in a much expanded version, in *The Paris Review*.

•

"The Cows" was also published as a chapbook by Sarabande Press (2011), with photographs by Theo Cote, Stephen Davis, and Lydia Davis.

"Eating Fish Alone" was also published by Madras Press (2013) in a chapbook in the "Stuffed Animals" series along with Harry Mathews's "Country Cooking from Central France."

The following "dream pieces" also appeared in *Proust, Blanchot, and the Woman in Red* (Cahier #5, Sylph Editions, Paris): "The Churchyard," "The Dog," "The Grandmother," "In the Gallery," "In the Train Station," "The Moon," "The Piano," "The Piano Lesson," "The Schoolchildren in the Large Building," "Swimming in Egypt," "The Woman in Red."

The following stories also appeared in the *Harper's Magazine* "Readings" section: "The Cornmeal," "Dinner," "The Dog Hair," "The Language of the Telephone Company," "The Song," "The Party," "Not Interested."

The following "Flaubert stories" also appeared in the *Harper's Magazine* "Readings" section: "Pouchet's Wife," "The Chairs," "The Coachman and the Worm," "The Visit to the Dentist," "The Cook's Lesson."

The following stories were reprinted in anthologies:
"Men" in *The Best American Poetry 2008* (ed. Wright) and *Old Flame: From the First 10 Years of 32 Poems Magazine.*
"Brief Incident in Short *a*, Long *a*, and Schwa" and "Ödön von Horváth Out Walking" in *Plume Anthology.*
"My Sister and the Queen of England" in *The Gertrude Stein Anthology.*
"Eating Fish Alone" in *Food and Booze: A Tin House Literary Feast.*

Note about the "dream pieces": Certain pieces which I am calling "dreams" were composed from actual night dreams and dreamlike waking experiences of my own; and the dreams, waking experiences, and letters of family and friends. I would like to thank individuals for the use of their dreams or waking experiences, as follows:

John Arlidge for "Swimming in Egypt"; Christine Berl for "The Piano Lesson"; Rachel Careau for "In the Gallery"; Tom and Nancy Clement, and Nancy's grandmother Ernestine, for "The Grandmother"; Claudia Flanders for "The Piano"; Rachel Hadas for "At the Bank" and "At the Bank: 2"; Paula Heisen for "The Sky Above Los Angeles"; and Edie Jarolim for "Ph.D." (which began as a "dream" and became shorter). The rest are my own.

Note about the "stories from Flaubert" and the "rant from Flaubert": The thirteen "stories from Flaubert" and the one "rant from Flaubert" were formed from material found in letters written by Gustave Flaubert, most of them to his friend and lover Louise Colet, during the period in which he was working on *Madame Bovary*. This material, contained in *Correspondance Volume II* (ed. Jean Bruneau; Editions Gallimard, 1980) and dating from 1853–54, was excerpted, translated from the French, and then slightly rewritten. My aim was to leave Flaubert's language and content as little changed as possible, only shaping the excerpt enough to create a balanced story, though I took whatever liberties I thought were necessary (in one case, for instance, combining material from two letters so that two related stories were turned into one; in another case, adding some factual material to a story to give more background to a character).

LYDIA DAVIS

THE END OF THE STORY

'It surprised me, over and over, to find that I was with such a young man. He was twenty-two when I met him. He turned twenty-three while I knew him, but by the time I turned thirty-five I did not know where he was anymore.'

Mislabelled boxes, confusing notes, wrong turnings – such are the obstacles in the way of the unnamed narrator of *The End of the Story* as she organizes her memories of a love affair into a novel. With compassion, wit and what seems to be candour, she seeks to determine what she actually knows about herself and her past, but we begin to suspect, along with her, that given the elusiveness of memory and understanding, any tale retrieved from the past must be fiction.

Back in print at last, this is Lydia Davis's first – and so far only – novel.

'Davis is a high priestess of the startling, telling detail. . . one of the best writers in America' Colm Tóibín

'Her work is exquisite, finely wrought and devastating. . . Read her now!' A. M. Homes

'Davis can invest descriptions of everyday events with startling reserves of emotion. She has a brilliant eye for the surprising, vibrant detail' *Sunday Times*

LYDIA DAVIS

THE COLLECTED STORIES OF LYDIA DAVIS

'Davis's short stories are perfected economies, witty devices, precision-made, primed to release intelligence, philosophy, hilarity. They celebrate the thinking universe while they redefine the possibilities of the form. There is no other writer quite like her' Ali Smith

Find out why fellow authors like Ali Smith, Dave Eggers and Jonathan Franzen love Lydia Davis's writing so much in this landmark collection of all of her stories to date from across three decades. And why James Wood described this book in the *New Yorker* as 'a body of work probably unique in American writing' and 'one of the great, strange American literary contributions'.

'What stories. Precise and piercing, extremely funny. Nearly all are unlike anything you've ever read' *Metro*

'Davis is a magician. Few writers working now make the words on the page matter more' Jonathan Franzen

'Remarkable. To read *Collected Stories* is to be reminded of the grand, echoing mind-chambers created by Sebald or recent Coetzee' *Independent*

'Brilliant, exciting, thrilling, extremely funny' *Daily Telegraph*